An Egg to Crack

by Stacy Davidowitz
Illustrations by Victoria Ying

AMULET BOOKS
NEW YORK

PUBLISHER'S NOTE: This is a work of fiction. Names, characters, places, and incidents are either the product of the author's imagination or used fictitiously, and any resemblance to actual persons, living or dead, business establishments, events, or locales is entirely coincidental.

Names: Davidowitz, Stacy, author. | Ying, Victoria, illustrator.
Title: An egg to crack / Stacy Davidowitz; illustrations by Victoria Ying.
Description: New York, NY: Amulet Books, 2018. | Series: Hanazuki; book 2
Identifiers: LCCN 2018001114 | ISBN 9781419729515 (hardback)
Subjects: | BISAC: JUVENILE FICTION / Readers / Chapter Books. | JUVENILE FICTION / Social Issues / Emotions & Feelings. | JUVENILE FICTION / Fantasy & Magic.
Classification: LCC PZ7.1.D3365 An 2018 | DDC [Fic]—dc23

Book design by Becky James

Printed and bound in China
10 9 8 7 6 5 4 3 2 1

ABRAMS The Art of Books
195 Broadway, New York, NY 10007
abramsbooks.com

CONTENTS

CHAPTER ONE

AN EGG OVER EASY

"Oh, hey there!" Hanazuki called, racing across a moon rock road to Kiazuki's side. It had been a minute since they'd hung out. Actually, three days' worth of minutes. Which was pretty unbelievable, considering Kiazuki was crashing with her on her moon. It was about time they spent some quality time together! *Small chat first, goop pedicures second.* "How are you liking your stay, my Moonflower sister?"

"Not your sister," Kiazuki said.

"*Technically* we don't know that."

"*Technically* we do. We were born from different moon spores."

"OK! Well, anything you need—a spare toothbrush, an extra pillow, a goop pedicure date with your non-Moonflower sister—just give me a holler!" Hanazuki took a big breath of fresh moon air and plopped down beside her squishy friends, the Hemka. Red Hemka and Yellow Hemka were wrestling. Orange Hemka was refereeing, gesturing madly with his ears. The rest were cheering them on. Well, except for Green Hemka. He was napping.

"You're not going to *do* anything?" Kiazuki asked, standing over her.

Hanazuki peered cautiously at the sky, afraid Kiazuki was referring to the Big Bad, a dark force that sapped moons of their color and beauty and made them go *KABLOOWEE*, but the sky was prettily dotted with stars and marshmallow clouds. Like it had been for weeks. Months, even. "Do something about what?" she replied.

"About *THAT*." Kiazuki pointed at the Hemka. Red was on Purple's shoulders and Yellow was on Lavender's shoulders, and they were chicken-fighting.

"*Riiight*," Hanazuki said, her head spinning for clarity. Did Kiazuki want her to show spectator spirit? Hoping that was it, she put two fingers in her mouth and whistled. "Go Red! Go Yellow! Sports, yeah!" Then she grinned and patted the space beside her, inviting Kiazuki to sit down. "You were right—now I feel like I'm doing my part! Come be a cheerleader with me!"

Kiazuki did not sit or cheer. She groaned. "That's obviously not what I meant."

"Cool, cool. So, what *did you*—?"

"Get control of your Hemka, Hanazuki! They're *fighting*. It's chaos. Isn't your job to, like, protect your moon?"

"Yeah, but . . ." She studied the Hemka. Red and Yellow were slapping each other silly. Red trash-talked Yellow: "CHOO CHEE POP POP GUH ZIG ZOG A *ZOW*!" Possible translation: "GET YOUR POPCORN READY, 'CAUSE I'M ABOUT TO PUT

ON A *SHOW*!" The most dangerous thing it did was provoke Hanazuki's craving for popcorn. "I think they're just playing," she said. "It's all in good fun!"

"Fine," Kiazuki retorted. "If you won't be the Moonflower your moon desperately needs, then I guess I'll have to do it for you." She stormed into the ring and plucked Red Hemka from Purple Hemka's shoulders. He shouted, "NAH NO NAH YAAAAA!" as Kiazuki carried him off with her toward a red Treasure Tree grove. "All in good fun, my Moonflower!" she shot back over her shoulder.

"So . . . are we still on for our goop pedicure?" Hanazuki called after her.

"We were never on for anything."

"I'll flash you my red toes later!"

Pink Hemka hopped into Red's place, and the wrestling match resumed. The other Hemka chanted, "GOO GAH HISS BOOOOYOO!" Pink Hemka just blew kisses at Hanazuki.

Hanazuki tried to enjoy the show, but no matter how many of Pink Hemka's air kisses she caught, she just wasn't feeling it. Why did Kiazuki always have to take the fun out of things? She might have been on a new, openhearted path, but on days like this, it felt like she was taking three leaps backward.

Hanazuki watched Pink Hemka defeat Yellow Hemka with a hug and felt an unexpected pang of guilt. No matter their differences, she couldn't let Kiazuki journey on her openhearted path alone. They could and would get through this. *Together.* And then they'd hug it out.

Hanazuki scrambled over to the red Treasure Tree grove and spotted Kiazuki and Red Hemka perched on a thick tree branch. "Hey, Kia—WHOA!" Hanazuki slipped in a goop puddle and landed flat on her back. "OOF!"

"Did a tree just fall?" Kiazuki wondered aloud. Before Hanazuki could so much as shout, "It's me—I'm a klutz—all's good," Kiazuki plowed on. "Whatever. What was I saying? Oh! So, the Big Bad disappears, and suddenly Hanazuki is all sunshine and rainbows?"

Hanazuki pushed herself up to her elbows. She could see Kiazuki holding Red, steam whistling from his ears. "GAH GRU ZEE ZAH!" he shouted.

"Exactly!" Kiazuki said. "It's like, here *I* am, doing my best to help, because *hello*, THE DANGER IS REAL, and all Hanazuki wants to do is *hang out.* I'd love to hang out. That sounds nice, but honestly, who's got time for that?"

"REE YEE YOO ZOO!"

"Hanazuki needs to know—a drama-free moon doesn't stay drama-free for long. When the climate is chill, Moonflowers drop their guard, and when Moonflowers drop their guard, BAM—everything falls apart."

"TEE TOO NAH NAH!"

Hanazuki felt her anger bubbling up. Here she was, letting Kiazuki crash on her moon in comfort for however long Kiazuki needed until she found a moon of her own to protect. Here she was, prepared to show Kiazuki unconditional support. Here she was, ready for a make-up hug. And this was how her Moonflower sister repaid her? By talking smack about her behind her back? To her own Alterling?

Hanazuki listened to Kiazuki rant on and on. Red kept shouting back at her. Surely, Kiazuki didn't think Red was actually siding with her, did she? She had to know that he was almost always in a *state of annoyance*, and she had to understand that his extra annoyed annoyance had been triggered when Kiazuki tore him away from his friends in the middle of a wrestling match . . . that he was winning! (Well, *maybe* winning. Yellow's ear-slapping was on point.) "It's OK to have fun once in a while!" Hanazuki blurted out. "Why can't you let yourself and everyone else on this moon have fun?!"

"Um." Kiazuki jumped down from the Treasure Tree and stared at Hanazuki. "What are you doing here? How long have you been *spying* on us?"

"I wasn't spying. Well, maybe I was. A little. Accidentally. 'Cause I fell."

"Uh-huh."

Hanazuki rose, wringing the goop from her skirt. "Look, it makes sense that you're feeling overprotective. If my moon had gotten destroyed by the Big Bad, I'd be just as freaked out as you are now."

"Me? I'm fine."

"But it's just as important to celebrate when things are good! Otherwise, what are we living for?" Hanazuki figured it was too early for a hug, so she took Kiazuki's hands and tried to twirl her around instead. "Let yourself have some fun! Let yourself have some fun *with me*!"

Kiazuki untangled herself from Hanazuki's hold. "Sorry to burst your bubble, but I'm not living for the opportunity to dance around the moon with you like *best friends forever*. Even if times are as good as you think they are, your advice is a moonsack of bologna!"

"What's bologna?"

Red Hemka started to shape-shift into a cold cut, but Kiazuki stopped him. She took a few seconds, then winced apologetically. "I'm being paranoid," she said to Hanazuki. "I probably overreacted about the wrestling match. Maybe the calm before the storm is just calm before . . . more calm. Right?"

Hanazuki smiled. "For sure."

Just then, the Treasure Trees ruffled with the vibration of Chicken Plant's screams. "IT'S HAPPENING, MOON PEOPLE! IT'S HAPPENING! I'M ABOUT TO POP. AN. EGG! WEEEEEEEELP!"

Hanazuki's heart leaped out of her chest. Red began to spin in circles.

"Uh, what are you both freaking out about?" Kiazuki asked. "Your moon is drama-free, chilltastic, good times, *blah, blah, blah*! And now, to boot, you're getting an adorable baby chick to celebrate."

"*Celebrate?*" Hanazuki repeated. Her mind was flashing with horrific memories of Chicken Plant's previous babies—demons out to destroy her moon. Should she run to Chicken Plant's side? Destroy the baby before it hatched? Mother the baby? Cage the baby? She looked at Red Hemka for an answer, but his ears were limp and his body was shaking. Oh, what should she do?!?

"Uh, moon to Hanazuki?" Kiazuki said, waving a hand in front of Hanazuki's face.

Hanazuki snapped back to reality and gripped Kiazuki's shoulders. "No, Kiazuki. Chicken Plant's babies are *not* worth celebrating. Like, at all. You've got to remember—we saw our first baby hatch together as we held him over the rim of an active volcano! We were about to toss him inside before he was born! That's how rotten he was supposed to turn out!"

Kiazuki rolled her eyes. "I remember everyone freaking out, but then the baby was born and he was *suuuuper* cute. Everyone had made this big to-do over nothing. Didn't he grow up in a snap and float off into the galaxy?"

"Yeah, he floated off. But *before* that, he was, well . . . less than an angel."

"How less?"

"He destroyed almost all of our Treasure Trees. He hacked them down like a woodpecker hopped up on treasure fruit candy."

Kiazuki's face scrunched in panic. "Have there been others?" she asked, grabbing Hanazuki's elbow and steering them toward Chicken Plant.

"There was Junior," Hanazuki replied. "He was so feisty that he made a Mazzadril fifty times his size run off to hide!"

"Wait, so do we know where the babies float off to?" Kiazuki asked. "Is there a destination, or are there a bunch of crazy chicken babies floating aimlessly in the galaxy?"

"Huh. I have no idea."

"Whatever. It doesn't matter where they go, as long as they *go*. All we need to worry about is the damage this baby will do while he's on your moon, and we'll want to get him to sprout that feather ASAP."

"Totally." Suddenly, a warm and fuzzy feeling washed over Hanazuki. Before she knew it, she'd dropped her head onto Kiazuki's shoulder and put her arms around her Moonflower sister.

Kiazuki froze. "Um, what are you doing?"

"I dunno. It's just, now that we're finally bonding—"

"This isn't bonding."

"—I feel better!"

"What? No. Don't feel better." Kiazuki pushed Hanazuki away from her. "Literally everything you're describing sounds like a nightmare."

"Exactly! And you know what's great about nightmares? You wake up from them! Plus, a little trouble keeps things interesting. Thanks for the motivational chitchat." Hanazuki flicked her wrist and snapped her fingers. "I've handled Chicken Plant's babies twice now, and I can do it again!"

"Sure you can." Kiazuki stormed ahead toward Chicken Plant, the moon dust kicking up at her heels.

Hanazuki felt her confidence crack. "Wait a sec," she said, jogging to Kiazuki's side. "You don't think I can handle this situation?"

Kiazuki stopped short. "The last two babies born on this moon were barely monsters. One hacked some trees—big deal. The other fought off a Mazzadril for you—basically saved your life. What are you going to do when an *actual* monster hatches?"

"Mother him? That worked well last time."

"Oh yeah? How long did you 'play mama'?"

"Hours . . . minutes . . . maybe five minutes."

"So, was it your mothering that made the babies into mild monsters . . . or luck?"

Hanazuki sucked in a deep breath. "OK, I see your point."

"Look, Sleepy Unicorn and Dazzlessence Jones and everyone else hyped up Chicken Plant's babies to be abominations because, back in the day, they probably were. This moon is overdue for a problem. I think we're about to see what a real terror Chicken Plant can egg up."

Hanazuki's stomach churned. "I guess. I hadn't thought it could get any worse."

"Things can *always* get worse," Kiazuki said. "For example, what if this baby is the LITERAL WORST? What if he *doesn't* sprout a feather and float off into the galaxy? What if he sticks around to destroy the whole moon? What if, at the end of the day, you end up moonless just like me?"

"I—I—I don't know."

"Exactly."

By the time they reached Chicken Plant, Hanazuki was a nervous wreck. So was Chicken Plant. Her feathers were sticking out in ten different directions. She was staring so hard at the egg quivering at the foot of her stalk that her eyes were beginning to cross. "Hold on to your Moodblossoms, buffoons," she said. "It's going to be a bumpy ride."

Just as Hanazuki's worry over the egg began to swell, Little Dreamer floated down to her in a chicken onesie, his eyes closed and his smile content like always. "Well, that's a little on the nose—er, beak," she said.

"Hee-haw shee-shuh."

"Cool, so, question," she said to him. "Why would the mooniverse drop this disaster at my doorstep just when things are on the up? Just when I've gotten Kiazuki to relax? Why?!"

Kiazuki cocked her chin.

"No offense." Hanazuki looked to Little Dreamer for an answer. But he dropped a treasure shaped like an egg, then zipped off—a chicken dot in the sky.

Just then, the egg started to crack.

Red Hemka growled at it. "GUH, GOO, GRRR."

Hanazuki felt her face get hot. She clenched and unclenched her fists. *No funny business, little guy, or you're gonna have me to deal with, and trust me, this mama won't be happy.*

A tiny pink beak peeked out. Then a blue wing. Then another blue wing. And then the eggshell fell away. Smiling up at Hanazuki was the most adorable chicken baby. He rolled around in a circle. Either he was missing feet or they were tucked underneath him. All of a sudden, he sprouted a single yellow . . . leg? Nope. Feather? Nope. It was a stalk!

Hanazuki gasped. Red Hemka's ears fell to the ground. Kiazuki looked back and forth between Hanazuki, who was speechless, and Chicken Plant, who was cooing and chirping at the baby Chicken Plant. "Uh . . . what's going on here?" Kiazuki finally asked.

"I have no idea," Hanazuki said, slowly shaking her head. "There's only one Chicken Plant. Except now there's . . . two."

"Welcome to the moon, my first baby Chicken Plant," Chicken Plant whispered, her eyes filled with hearts. "I think I'll call you . . . Tenders."

Is this good? Hanazuki wondered. *Is it worse than bad?* Chicken Plant had always had chicks. That's just how it was. But now she had a baby Chicken Plant. What in the moon did that mean?

CHAPTER TWO

TENDERS

"*Happy Day of Birth to you, Our Chicklet Plant so cute! Happy Day of Birth, Dear Tenders, Happy Day of Birth to you!*" The whole moon crew—Hanazuki, Kiazuki, Red Hemka, Dazzlessence Jones, Sleepy Unicorn, Doughy Bunington, Maroshi, Wanderer, Kiyoshi, Zikoro, and the rest of the Hemka—broke into wild applause.

"Regarding Tenders," Dazzlessence Jones whispered to Hanazuki, "so far, so good."

Hanazuki gave Dazz a thumbs-up. Tenders *was* cute. *Heart-meltingly* cute. But would he *stay* cute? The singing, the attention, the enthusiasm—it was all part of their plan. If they nurtured the baby Chicken Plant, then *maaaaybe* he wouldn't destroy her moon.

"Who's hungry?" Hanazuki asked, bringing out a cake in the shape of a chicken tender. A BABY CHICKEN PLANT SHOWER FOR TENDERS! 0 LB., 3 OZ. HAPPY, HEALTHY, NOT A MONSTER was written in white icing. A single candle flickered.

Chicken Plant awkwardly patted her son's back with her wing. "Make a wish, kid."

Tenders drew in a shallow breath. "I wish that—"

"But don't spill it," she cut in. "Lock the wish in that pebble brain of yours, and then, well, if you're lucky, it'll come true."

"OK, Mama Chick P. I'm gonna make the bestest, most secretest wish in the world!"

"Quickly. Then flap out the flame, 'cause it sure as feathers ain't gonna flap itself out."

Tenders flapped his little wings, pushing air at the candle until it went dark.

The whole group cheered. "YAAAAY!"

Hanazuki collected cake crumbs and tossed them toward Tenders's beak. He caught some with a "Yum!" Others smacked him in the face. "Hee hee hee!" he laughed adorably. "That's silly! Auntie H, you're silly." Hanazuki's heart grew a size.

"*Tenders be lit, oh baby!*" Dazzlessence Jones sang. "Yo, Tendy, you remember my name, too? Here's a hint. I'm not your aunt, but your—"

"Dunkle!"

"Ha! OK, Dunkle what?" Dazzlessence struck

three poses—a squat, a ninja kick, a handstand—to show off his dazzle essence in different light.

"Dunkle Diamond. Pretty sparkle. More."

Dazzlessence pushed out his chest and beat it with his fists. "More? You want more of this shine? *Exhale on me, baby!*" Tenders took a deep breath in through his nose and out through his beak. "Now feather-dust me!" Tenders wiped Dazz's diamond with his downy feathers. "*How shiny is that? Top of the line shiny, yeeeeah!*" Tenders's eyes sparkled in amazement.

"You think that's dazzling?" Sleepy Unicorn drawled. From his horn, he zapped Dazzlessence Jones with a bolt of lightning magic. "*Oh baby, hot, hot, hot!*" Dazz sang, splashing his behind with treasure fruit juice.

Tenders giggled. "Magic me love. Magic is sleepy fun!"

Sleepy nodded. "It sure is, Tenders Plant Chicken thing, it sure is. Now I'd like to teach you something very important that was taught to me when I was a young 'corn. Firstly—*Zzzzzz.*" Sleepy collapsed onto his belly, hooves out, and erupted into snores.

"Hee hee hee!" Tender laughed. "Wake up, Unicuncle Sleepy!

"Yeah, bro, not gonna happen," Maroshi said, approaching the group with his favorite Flochi, Wanderer, perched on his shoulder. "The sleepy corn's sweet-dreamin' his way through the galaxy. Anyway, I can't believe it's only been hours since you cracked your way to freedom. Gnarly journey, I imagine. Respect." Maroshi gave him the shaka sign, curling his three middle fingers and leaving his thumb and pinky extended. Tenders copied him, giving the shaka sign right back. "We all thought you'd be a monster, so this is a real treat. Stay cool, T."

Tenders cocked his chin. Hanazuki elbowed Maroshi.

"Never mind," Maroshi said, flinging his arm around Tenders. "All right, T. You're stuck in the soil, that's your toil, but don't you fret. I'm gonna help you to simulate flying!" He whipped his surfboard out from under his arm and placed it below Tenders's belly. "Spread your wings, bro. Lean onto the board. Move *that* way and *that* way and *that* way. Groovy aviation!"

After Tenders had his third faux-flying wipeout, Kiyoshi stepped in nervously. "Hey, nice partay, T. Don't want to take up too much of your time—you're kind of a celebrity and sort of unpredictable—but I just want to tell you that I see stuff."

"Arg?" Tenders looked up and down and around, confused.

"I mean, we *all* see stuff," he explained. "But I see the past, the present, and the future in black treasure fruit. And from what I can see"—he squinted at a black Treasure Tree just a few feet away—"this mooniverse has got 'out of this moon' plans for you! It has to do with, um . . ." He squinted at the tree again. "Family."

"*Family?*" Chicken Plant squawked. "I'm Tenders's family. You're telling me, Mr. I See Stuff, that there are 'out of this moon' plans in store for *us*?" Kiyoshi made an "M" sound for "Maybe," but Chicken Plant screeched over him. "Like what? Unlimited cake? 'Cause that would be excellent for Tenders's bone growth. Also, my appetite. A hungry mama can't be expected to mother, you know."

"Cool. Yeah. I dunno." Kiyoshi darted his eyes between a few other black Treasure Trees in the distance. "It's not totally clear what's going to happen, and I only have a 50 percent success rate, so . . ."

"No cake?" Chicken Plant asked him.

"Probably not unlimited," Kiyoshi replied.

"Sounds to me like a crock of comet stew!"

Chicken Plant exclaimed. "Tenders, be wary of fortune-tellers. In my experience, they're scamming for eggs."

"Yes, Mama," Tenders said. "Uncle Kiyoshi, do you see eggs and scam?"

"Do you mean eggs and ham?" Kiyoshi asked.

"What's ham?" Tenders asked.

While Dazzlessence and Maroshi cracked up, and Kiyoshi laughed awkwardly with them, Hanazuki helped herself to some cake. All the talk of it had made her hungry! She sat down at a picnic table to enjoy a slice, and watched Tenders from afar. He seemed to be getting smarter and sweeter and more fun by the second. None of Chicken Plant's previous chicks had lasted this long without wreaking havoc. Maybe Tenders wouldn't become a threat after all!

Hanazuki tried to relax. Everyone seemed to be having a great time. Maroshi's Flochis were swimming through the air like a school of fish, playing Guess the Leader. Half of the Hemka were shape-shifting into toys for Tenders, and the other half were playing with the toys. Zikoro had taken on the role of Tenders's number one fan and protector—he was up against the back of Tenders's stalk with his fangs bared. *But . . .* where was Kiazuki?

"Kiazuki?" Hanazuki called into the crowd. No response. She left her slice of cake and wandered to the outskirts of the party. She kept waiting until she made it all the way inside a Treasure Tree grove. "Kiazuki? Are you here?" Nothing. She checked the Safety Cave. She checked the area where Kiazuki had set up camp. She checked with Talking Pyramid to see if he had seen her, but he had no idea. Kiazuki was nowhere to be found.

Hanazuki was seriously starting to worry when, all of a sudden, Little Dreamer flew down with a chicken-shaped treasure. "Thanks, little dude. Also feel like dropping me a hint as to where Kiazuki is? Did you see her on your way down?"

"Wazee wee wee," he whispered.

"That's OK. Figured I'd ask. I don't get why Kiazuki has disappeared! We all thought Tenders was going to be a terror, but he's so cute! Does she think his cuteness is all a front? Does she think he's going to *mature* into a terror?"

"Wazza wee."

"Wait! Did seeing a new baby make her sad? Did it remind her of her lost Zikoros? Did her dark thoughts bring her to the Dark Side of the Moon! Oh moonshakes, that had to be it!"

Little Dreamer flipped and then flew off over a Mouth Portal.

"Thanks, snoozy man! I feel better already!" Hanazuki leaped inside the Mouth Portal and was instantly transported to the Dark Side of the Moon. She immediately saw Kiazuki heading toward a cave. Not just *any* cave! The cave of Basal Ganglia, a maniacal brain with eyeballs who wanted to take over the moon. "KIAZUKI, *NOOOOOO*!!!"

Kiazuki froze, then slowly turned around.

"Hey," she said to Hanazuki, like a Mazzadril caught in sunshine. "What are you doing here?"

"Looking for you! What are *you* doing here?"

"Um." Kiazuki's eyes darted around. "I was just, uh . . ."

"Looking for some alone time?" Hanazuki placed a gentle hand on her shoulder. "It's OK, I get it. Big parties aren't for everyone, especially ones celebrating a cute little newbie to the moon. I can see how that might be hard for you."

Kiazuki cocked an eyebrow.

"But just a heads-up—you're not going to be alone with your thoughts inside that cave. That's where Basal Ganglia lives, and in case you don't remember, that brain's crazy."

"I CAN HEAR YOU, MY UNFAITHFUL SUBJECT," Basal Ganglia shouted.

"NOT YOUR SUBJECT," Hanazuki shouted back, then made circles with her finger around her temple.

"Well, maybe I'm not looking to be alone with

my thoughts," Kiazuki said. "Maybe I'm looking for advice."

Huh? Hanazuki took a second, then another second, trying to wrap her head around what she'd just heard. How was it that Kiazuki would consult a scheming maniac over a fellow Moonflower, sister or not? It didn't make any sense!

"Great talk," Kiazuki said. "I'm gonna go now."

"Wait!" Hanazuki cried. "Look, don't be scared or upset about Tenders. In an eggshell, he's really fun and silly and sweet, and I bet he'll stay that way. I also bet he could come up with a funny nickname for you, like 'Auntie Kiazuki.'"

"That's not a nickname. You just added 'Auntie.'"

"'Kooky Kiazuki,' then?"

Kiazuki rolled her eyes. "I'm not afraid of Tenders. I'm afraid *for* him. Do you *really* think Chicken Plant is going to be a good mom? Is this moon really the best place for him?"

"So, that's why you're here? To get advice on how best to look after Tenders?"

"Duh."

Hanazuki sighed with enormous relief. It was so cool to see Kiazuki act with such compassion! "Don't worry, Moonflower *friend.* I think that with the entire moon's help, Tenders will be just fine. I mean, everyone likes him, and he likes everyone, too. You can ask Basal all the questions you want, but don't be alarmed if he gives you crooked advice."

"YOU'RE A CROOKED SPICE," shouted Basal.

"Oh boy." Hanazuki smiled at Kiazuki. "Anyway, when you're done, come back to the party. I'll save you a slice of cake. Actually, the cake was *very* popular. It might be goners. Do you like churros?"

"Who doesn't?" Kiazuki replied.

Hanazuki returned to the Light Side of the Moon to find Tenders surrounded by his guests. She joined the huddle and watched with

amazement as he performed the ultimate party trick—spinning a pacifier in his beak! He pushed the pacifier forty-five degrees and then another forty-five degrees and then another and another until it was right-side up. A baby bird genius!

A few moments later, Red Hemka pushed through the crowd, with a rainbow-colored pacifier made up of nine shape-shifted Hemka.

Hanazuki grinned. Finally, the Hemka had decided on a toy for Tenders and were going to let *him* play with it! She waited a couple of seconds for Red to hand the pacifier over to Tenders, but Red just held on. He began to count down, "WUN, WOO, WEE." Then, just like Tenders's party trick, Red's pacifier began to spin.

Tenders was so amazed, he couldn't look away. He went cross-eyed, dropped his pacifier, and thrust his wings out for balance.

"Hey, slow down, Red," Hanazuki urged. "This is cute and all, but I don't want Tenders to get sick."

But Red's pacifier didn't slow down. It spun

faster, faster, faster. He seemed to be waiting for something. Applause? Hanazuki didn't applaud—she couldn't! All she could do was stand there horrified as Tenders's focus narrowed in. Red applauded himself. He darkened to the shade of ketchup, then hot sauce. He appeared possessed, like a demon had taken control of his squishy little body.

Tenders finally covered his eyes with his wings and began to cry-chirp.

"Knock it off," Hanazuki scolded Red. "Are you *trying* to scare Tenders? You're the leader of the pack. If you can't stop the pacifier, get the other Hemka to."

The pacifier spun at the frequency of a high-speed fan.

Tenders's feathers flapped at his face.

"SERIOUSLY, RED! WHAT'S WRONG WITH YOU?"

Just then, Chicken Plant plucked the giant pacifier from Red's mouth. She tossed it to the ground, and the Hemka tumbled back into their normal squishy selves. Red started to explain, but Chicken Plant ate him whole. The crowd gasped as he pressed against her insides, screaming. Chicken Plant yelled, "Bitter. Phooey. Ow," until, finally, she popped an egg. Red instantly cracked out of the shell.

Hanazuki ran to help him, but he pushed her away and stormed off into a nearby red Treasure Tree grove. "REALLY?!" she called after him. "You're mad at *ME*? Reckless leadership has consequences! And sometimes, those consequences include getting eaten by Chicken Plant!"

Hanazuki brushed it off. Red could go off and be angry for a little while. She was going to focus on the party. Soon it was time for presents: compostable diapers from Maroshi, stalk decor from Teal Hemka, a bedazzled cowboy hat from Dazzlessence Jones. Hanazuki volunteered to put together a list of gift givers and their gifts so that

Chicken Plant could refer to it later for thank-you notes. Even though Chicken Plant protested, squawking, "What a waste of time. You're using a feather pen, which is insulting to my kind. We didn't *ask* for presents," Hanazuki did it anyway. She still couldn't shake the episode with Red and needed the distraction.

While Chicken Plant and Tenders modeled matching mama/chick sleeping masks from Sleepy Unicorn, Hanazuki noticed Kiazuki crouched on the ground, whispering into Tenders's ear. She'd come back from the Dark Side of the Moon, and look at all that compassion! "Whatcha talking about, you two?"

Tenders pulled down the sleeping mask, revealing bulging eyes. "We were—"

"Learning a joke," Kiazuki cut in. "From me. I was teaching it."

"Ooh! Let's hear it," Hanazuki said. She waved at the crowd. "Guys, Kiazuki and Tenders have a joke for us!"

Everyone waited for something funny to fly out of either of their mouths.

"Loud and proud, K!" Maroshi encouraged, his fist out for a bump. "Shy don't fly!"

"I'm not shy," Kiazuki said, ignoring his fist. "Since when have I ever been shy?"

"Well, you've certainly never been funny," Sleepy said, mid-yawn. "Maybe you're being shy because teaching jokes is a new experience. I'd be shy if I had to teach insomnia."

"That's ridiculous!" Kiazuki said. "I'm hilarious, and so is Tenders, and if you want proof, I'll give you proof! Flex your funny bones, because this duo is about to crush." She paused, then asked Tenders, "Why did the Chicken Plant cross the road?"

"He, um, can't," Tenders replied with hesitation. "He's rooted too hard in the ground."

"Ha! Ha! Ha!" Kiazuki slapped her thigh. "See? Hysterical!"

It wasn't hysterical, but Hanazuki didn't want to

insult Kiazuki. She tricked herself into laughing, as Sleepy Unicorn fell dead asleep at the punch line. "Ha! Oh, Kiazuki! Oh, Tenders! Comedians *indeed*. Get these two their own comedy special!"

Chicken Plant clanked a pebble against a raised glass of rainbow waterfall—*ding, ding, ding!*—and said, "Moving on. I'd like to propose a toast." The crowd hushed and raised their glasses of rainbow waterfall. Chicken Plant continued. "Now, I've never grown attached to any of my chicks—nicest thing they've ever done for me was leave. But this little guy—my Tenders—he's special. Not just in my eyes, but in the eyes of statistics."

"*Statistics, yeah, so hot right now,*" Dazzlessence sang, raising the roof.

"Here's a history lesson for all of you," Chicken Plant went on. "There are two breeds: chickens and Chicken Plants. Chickens, well, you've seen them. They're dumb jerks. Chicken *Plants*, though. Not dumb jerks. Plus, they make up only 1 percent of hatched eggs! That means for every ninety-nine dumb jerk chickens, there is 1 not-dumb-jerk Chicken Plant. Tenders is a total rarity. However, had you told me yesterday that I'd pop a plant, I'd still have said, 'Well, he sure as the Big Bad ain't rooting himself near me. I've only mothered for a day at a time, and even that's given me gray feathers around my mouth.'"

Tenders snuck a peek at Chicken Plant's mouth.

"I see you, Tenders."

"Sorry."

"The point is, when life gives you a Chick Plant, you throw a Chick Plant shower. My son's eyes are big and his beak is small, and going by the books, that's cute. Cute is good. It helps lure the Hemka, and then I get to eat the Hemka. Preferably the sweet ones like Yellow and Pink. Not Red. He was bitter and gross."

The Hemka huddled together in horror. Hanazuki shook her head.

"I digress. Oh, Tenders!" Chicken Plant began to choke up. Hanazuki began to choke up, too. It was the most moving speech imaginable . . . for Chicken Plant. "Cheers!" she finally said, raising her glass even higher.

"Cheers!" the moon creatures responded, slamming back their glasses of rainbow waterfall.

After that, everyone partied hard. Following the forty-sixth Chicken Dance and more cake, Hanazuki felt herself fading. She happily hugged her friends good night and went to bed. As she snuggled inside her sleeping bag, her eyes fluttered shut. She dreamed only of Tenders and the boundless joy he was going to bring to the mooniverse!

Hours later, Hanazuki was startled awake. The ground shook. The Treasure Trees shook, too. She threw herself out of bed, listening to Chicken Plant's screams echo furiously through the atmosphere. "HELP! HELP! TENDERS HAS BEEN CHICKNAPPED!"

CHAPTER THREE

THE INVESTIGATION BEGINS!

I'M COMING, CHICKEN PLANT!" Hanazuki shouted, leaping through a series of Mouth Portals to the scene of the crime. Upon arrival, she put her hands on her knees, doubled over with a cramp.

Thankfully, Dazzlessence Jones was already beside Chicken Plant and jotting down her testimony in a spiral notebook. "So, tell me," he said, flipping through dozens of self-portraits and sheriff reports until he came to a blank page. "Where did you last see Tenders?"

"Here," Chicken Plant said.

Dazzlessence popped a wad of gum into his mouth. “Can you be more specific?”

“Seriously?” Chicken Plant flapped her wing at a shallow hole in the moon earth beside her. “That’s where Tenders was rooted. None of this is new information.”

“*Interesting*,” Dazzlessence sang. He stretched the gum out from his mouth and twirled it around his finger. “And where were you when the crime was committed?”

“*RIGHT HERE*, YOU IDIOT.”

“Do you have an alibi?”

“An ali-*WHAT?*”

“*An alibi, bye, bye*,” Dazzlessence sang, then popped the gum back into his mouth. “A moon creature who can vouch for you.”

“I can vouch for her,” Hanazuki blurted out, lifting her head from between her knees. “Chicken Plant never moves. You know that. She had to have been right here the whole time.”

"*Interesting*," Dazzlessence sang as he circled Chicken Plant. "So you admit you were at the crime scene when the crime was committed?"

"Sure, but I was sleeping. Do you need me to spell that out for you, too? It's when you close your eyes and you're out until breakfast."

Dazzlessence studied his notebook, tapping the pen against his diamond head. "I don't know, CP . . ."

Chicken Plant pounced at Dazzlessence's notebook and ate it whole.

"Whoa, whoa, whoa! You just ate three weeks of sketches and sheriff reports!" He produced his badge, which read: DAZZ, DIAMOND DETECTIVE AND SELF-PORTRAIT ARTIST. "I kindly ask that you follow my orders. Birth my notebook and answer the rest of my—"

"We are FINITO with the quack questions," Chicken Plant broke in. "Go out and find my Tenders already, you DUMB DIAMOND! I want a SEARCH PARTY! I want MISSING: CHICK PLANT posters! I want THE BEST REWARDS offered! FIND THE CHICKNAPPER NOW!"

"Hey," Hanazuki said, wedging herself between them. "Let's take a deep breath, you two. It's OK, Chicken Plant. Of course you didn't chicknap your own son. I saw you when Tenders was born. You had hearts in your eyes."

"No, I didn't."

"Yes, you did."

"Hearts? Blech. I so much as see a heart and I practically vomit."

"Well, then, what's the big fuss all about?" Hanazuki asked. "Why else would you want him back?"

"I DON'T WANT HIM BACK!" Chicken Plant popped an egg. It cracked open, revealing Dazzlessence's notebook. She ranted on. "You've seen my other offspring. They always seem cutesy-tootsey when they're first born, but give it a day and they become absolute nutcases. You

want Tenders to destroy our moon?! Find him before it's too late! This is not my problem. It's YOUR problem."

Hanazuki handed Dazzlessence his gooey notebook. "Let's get Tenders back to us. I already miss the little guy."

"Me, too. Who else is going to call me Dunkle Diamond?"

"Probably no one. Wanna spearhead this investigation together?"

"You got it, Ace."

"LESS WEIRD DETECTIVE TALK," Chicken Plant screeched. "MORE INVESTIGATION."

"Where do you think we should start?" Hanazuki asked Dazz.

Chicken Plant answered for him, "YOU SEE THE HEMKA OVER THERE? START WITH THEM. CHOP-CHOP."

"On it!" Hanazuki and Dazzlessence said together. They rushed over to all ten Hemka, who were bathing in Rainbow Swirl Lake.

"Hey, early risers," Hanazuki greeted them. "Did you hear that Tenders is missing?" They nodded sleepily. "That's great, because—"

"We are on to YOU!" Dazzlessence interjected.

The Hemka looked up in confusion. "YA-YOO GAKKA?"

"Stop colluding. Mouths closed. Ears up," Dazz commanded. The Hemka, still in the lake, raised their ears above their heads. "Now listen up, Hemka. Every creature's guilty until proven innocent."

"Um, I think you've got that backward," Hanazuki whispered to Dazz. "Every creature's *innocent* until proven *guilty*."

"Nope." Dazzlessence spun, showing off his sparkle. "I'm the Shiny Cop. You're the Good Cop. Go with it."

Hanazuki's mind flooded with questions, but Dazzlessence was already directing the Hemka out of the lake and into a line. "*Mug shot tiiiiime!*" He flipped to the back of his notebook, wiped the egg-white goo from the page, and began sketching each of his suspects. When he'd finished, he slammed his notebook shut and paced up and down the line like a drill sergeant. "Fill me in, Hemka. What leads have you got on Tenders's whereabouts?"

Red stepped forward in a salute. "ZA HAT DUG WIT KROW NWANZ WIN GUZ."

Dazzlessence began to jot it down and then paused on "WIT." "I forgot that I don't speak Hemka." He faced Hanazuki. "Can you translate, partner?"

"Sure!" She crouched down in front of Red. "Hey, buddy. I know we had a rough day yesterday, but you think you can help us out? Any idea who might have taken Tenders?"

He rolled his eyes like, *Duh, I just told you*, then repeated himself. "ZA HAT DUG WIT KROW NWANZ WIN GUZ."

"Cool . . . That's a great lead . . ." She paused. "Actually, I'm still lost."

Red repeated himself a third time, and when that left Hanazuki scratching her head again, he began hopping up and down, annoyed. He pulled the other Hemka into a huddle. "ZOO ZA GREE CHA-CHA YOO-YA. GRU YA-ZOO YA?" he asked them. They made some weird untranslatable noises and then stood in a semicircle around Red Hemka, waiting for their cue. He waved his ear at them, and they began to shape-shift, charades-style:

(a) Red Hemka, Orange Hemka, and Yellow Hemka fused their bodies and danced like a flame. *Fire!*

(b) In sync and bum to bum, Purple Hemka and Pink Hemka walked on their ears, like a medium-sized animal with four legs. Lavender Hemka morphed into the tail. Lime Green Hemka lay belly-down on top of them with his tongue hanging out. He panted. *Puppy!*

(c) Teal Hemka pointed to the flower on Hanazuki's head. *Mood plume!*

(d) Blue Hemka and Yellow Hemka scrunched their faces and flapped their ears. *Cute bugs!*

The Hemka morphed back into their normal squishy selves. Red stood tall with pride and waited for Hanazuki to put it all together. She tried really hard, slowly saying, "'*Look for a fire puppy with a mood plume who wants cute bugs.*'"

Red slumped over.

"What did *you* see?" Hanazuki asked Dazz.

"I saw '*A fiery mini-elephant with hair flaps,*'" Dazz said. "Do we know any chicknapping fiery mini-elephants with hair flaps?"

"No. I don't know any elephants at all."

They both looked at Red. He was ear-slapping himself. "GRU GA SA-SA!" he shouted at the Hemka, ordering them back into a huddle. It was taking a long time. Dazzlessence tapped his cowboy boots against the moon earth, waiting for a fresh charade. Hanazuki tried to wait patiently, too, but quickly realized she was digging her fingernails into her palms.

"QUIT STANDING AROUND!" Chicken Plant screamed in the distance. "FIND TENDERS! NOW!"

"Forget it, Red," Hanazuki said. "If you can't get the Hemka to shape-shift into something helpful right this instant, we've got to move on."

Red morphed into a ketchup bottle.

"C'mon, this is no time for games."

Red morphed into a jar of sauerkraut.

"Not funny, Red!"

Dazzlessence tugged at Hanazuki's elbow. "This is a *waaaaste of time, oh baby!*"

"I know. Sorry." They began to walk away, but Red wrapped his ears around Hanazuki's arm. "GREE GRAH ZU CHEE YOO!"

Hanazuki peeled him from her forearm and laid him on the ground. "You're not helping, Red! I can't stand here all day trying to figure out what you mean! If you have something to say, FIGURE IT OUT with the other Hemka and TELL ME LATER."

Red began flapping his ears against the moon earth, tantrum-style.

"DID YOU FIND TENDERS?" Chicken Plant squawked. "ASKING FOR A FRIEND."

"Tell your friend, '*Not yet!*'" Dazz sang back.

"WELL, GET ON IT, YOU PAIR OF POLICING NUMBSKULLS."

As Hanazuki jogged off, she felt her cheeks

getting hot. Thanks to Red and their own failed policing, she and Dazz had just wasted precious time. They needed to step up their game STAT for Tenders, for Chicken Plant, for the safety of the moon! BUT HOW?! Hanazuki's panic spiral was suddenly curtailed by Little Dreamer, who flew by in a onesie the many colors of fire. "Woozie woo wa," he whispered, dropping her a treasure the shape of a mini hotdog.

"Thanks," Hanazuki said flatly, tucking it into her back pocket. Then, as Little Dreamer zipped ahead, she realized he might be able to help. "Snoozy dude, wait!" she called, racing to meet him. "My partner and I are on a mission to find Tenders. He's been chicknapped. The Hemka were useless. I know it's a long shot, but any ideas?"

"Woo-wee-wah."

"Yeah, us neither. I mean, who would have motivation to chicknap Tenders? Is there a moon creature who has something against Chicken

Plant? A moon creature who craves chicken meat? A moon creature who has no self-control?"

"Dah shah tah." Without warning, Little Dreamer floated off into the sky, leaving Hanazuki all alone with her spinning thoughts. *A moon creature who has something* against *Chicken Plant. Who craves chicken meat. Who has no self-control.*

Something clicked. "THAT'S GOT TO BE IT!"

Dazzlessence lurched forward to her side. "Who? Where? What?"

"No. I mean, I think I know what the Hemka were trying to tell us. '*A hotdog with a crown who wants chicken wings!*'"

Dazzlessence swallowed his gum whole. "Are you thinking what I'm thinking?"

"Next stop: Doughy Bunington."

CHAPTER FOUR

THE PLOT THICKENS

"We so appreciate your cooperation," Hanazuki told Doughy Bunington as she took a seat across from him at a picnic table on the Dark Side of the Moon. Dazzlessence Jones paced menacingly around the table, and dodging the former's stomping cowboy boots was Red Hemka, who'd followed them to the interrogation without so much as a grunt.

"Cooperation is key for a cook," Doughy said, pointing to himself. "Both start with 'coo' for a reason."

Doughy Bunington didn't cook treats so much

as he farmed them, but Hanazuki wasn't about to pick a fight. "That's a fun fact," she said instead, leaning into her "Good Cop" role. "So, if it's not too much trouble, we have just a few questions for you."

"And I have just a few *croissants* for *you*!" Doughy tore the napkin cover off a bowl of croissants, except it was just a bowl. There were no croissants inside.

Hanazuki forced a smile and joked, "Should we use our imagination?"

"This is not a game," he said. "Go on into the field, Hanazuki. Pick some fresh ones for the table."

Hanazuki did everything in her power not to snort. "With all due respect," she said, "we don't *need* croissants, and I certainly don't have time to collect them. This is an urgent matter."

"You can't expect me to answer urgent questions on an empty stomach now, can you?"

Hanazuki's smile dropped. "Of course not." She

went out into the field and plucked the first three croissants she could find, then rushed back to the picnic table.

Dazzlessence was staring with suspicion at Doughy's bulging belly. "Empty stomach you say?" he asked.

Hanazuki knew he was implying that Doughy's belly was filled with Tenders. She'd noticed it bulging too, but had hoped it was just gas.

Doughy sniffed the croissants. "Empty as a cave that's empty," he said.

Dazzlessence narrowed his eyes. "Hanazuki, what do you think about Doughy's claim that he's running on an *empty stomach*?"

Red, who'd been strangely silent this whole time, tried to insert himself into the detective duo. He raised one ear to Hanazuki as if giving her a thumbs-up, then turned to Doughy and dropped his other ear as if giving him a thumbs-down. Then, he leaped onto Doughy's face and pried his mouth open.

"*AHHHHHHH!*" Doughy screamed.

"Whoa! Red! Stop!" Hanazuki cried.

Red didn't stop. He stuck his ear down Doughy's throat and fished around for evidence.

"Hey! I'm talking to you!" Hanazuki grabbed Red and dropped him to the ground. "Dude, you can't *attack* the suspects. Dazz and I have got this."

Doughy massaged his jaw. Then, wasting no time at all, he bit into a croissant.

Hanazuki turned her attention back to Dazz. "I don't think we should jump to any conclusions," she said. "If Doughy says his stomach is empty, it's empty. After all, Mr. Bunington is a highly regarded moon denizen."

"Of *course* he is," Dazzlessence said. "All highly regarded moon denizens are exiled and sentenced to life on the Dark Side of the Moon. *Riiiiight?*"

"That's right, I'm a good hotdog," Doughy said, unbothered, croissant crumbs flying from his lips. "I'll explain my eating habits more. My stomach is *always* empty because I never get full. Thank the pastry gods that 'stuffed' is a feeling I've never experienced. What is it like? Just thinking about it makes me want to curl up near a fire and bawl my eyes out."

Dazzlessence slammed his fist onto the table. "Quit jerking us around and tell us *WHY* your belly is bulging! WHAT ARE YOU HIDING?!"

Doughy rubbed his belly guiltily. "All right. You caught me. I had a blueberry donut binge for breakfast and then a scone sampling for mid-morning snack. They were so good that my body won't relieve them. Compliments to the chef! That's me. I'm the chef."

"We *know*," Dazzlessence sang.

"And yet, I'm starving! Do you hear my hunger pangs?"

Hanazuki leaned close to Doughy's belly. It rumbled like an approaching stampede of goats. "Wow, someone get this hotdog more food."

Red was on it. He rushed into the pastry farm.

"Savory, please," Doughy called after him. "Bacon cheddar! No, Bolognese brisket! No, chicken adobe!"

"Aha!" Dazzlessence said, shoving his finger in Doughy's face. "*Chicken!*"

"Chicken?" Doughy chuckled. "No, you misunderstand me. I said, 'chai kin.' Sounds the same, tastes different. Chai kin means 'a spice in the same family as chai.' Like cardamom."

"That sounds like a *lie*," Dazz said.

"The proof is in the pudding." Doughy reached inside his bun and pulled out a cup of chocolate pudding. Just then, Red returned, recklessly tossing six cupcakes onto the table. They tumbled into Hanazuki's lap, and the icing globbed onto her skirt.

"Really, Red?!" she said, putting the cupcakes back on the table. "You couldn't be more careful?"

"Thank you, Red thing," Doughy said, admiring his buffet. "In theory, this should be enough food."

"It is," Dazz said.

"But forget *hungry.* All this confrontation is getting me *hangry.* That's hungry plus angry. I feel like I'm being interviewed for *MoonTop Chef.*"

"You're not," Dazz said.

"That's what they'd like me to believe." Doughy devoured four cupcakes in a single bite. "Their producers like to go undercover."

Dazz drilled down on the suspect. "Where were you LAST NIGHT at the CRACK OF MOON?" he demanded.

"Sleeping," Doughy answered. "No, night farming. No, night eating. No, sleeping."

"Were you 'sleeping' on the Dark Side or the Light Side?"

"Both? I sleepwalk, so it's hard for me to say."

"Aha!"

"Aha *what*? Did I *win*? Am I *on the show*?" Doughy rammed the last two cupcakes into his mouth. "If you're taking me somewhere, I'm going to need donuts. If you're not taking me somewhere, I'm going to need donuts. My brain requires fuel—*beep beep!*"

"Fine!" Hanazuki interjected, then raced through the pastry farm again. She plucked two donuts and then turned back, bumping right into

Red! He was carrying donuts, too, and they fell out of his ears and onto her feet. Meanwhile, the donuts she was carrying smashed against her top. "UGH, RED! COME ON! NOT AGAIN!"

"GAH FRU ZEE," he said. He tried to brush the crumbs off of her, but was only rubbing in the oil stains, making it a whole lot worse.

Hanazuki shooed him off. "You're messing everything up. Why don't you get some rest?"

Red lay on top of an apple strudel and pretended to sleep. Then he popped back up with a high five, and accidentally flung a piece of apple strudel at Hanazuki's head.

"What is wrong with you?!" Hanazuki shouted. "Take a breather. Waaaaay over there." She directed him to a mushroom on the other side of the pastry farm, then plucked two more donuts and headed back to the picnic table alone. Why had Red followed her here? Was he trying to mess up the investigation? Keep Tenders away from them?

Dazzlessence grabbed the donuts from Hanazuki and brought them to Doughy.

"Oh, goodie!" Doughy clapped. "These are my newest invention—French crullers stuffed with pumpkin spice custard. Haven't even tried them yet!" He went in for a chomp, but Dazzlessence crumbled the donuts in his fist and tossed them at Doughy's forehead. "*NOOOOOOOOOOOOOOO!*"

"That's the price you pay," Dazz said, wiping his crumby hands on Doughy's bun. "And this is just the beginning. Things are about to get a lot nastier unless, of course, you CONFESS."

"Confess?" Doughy whimpered. "Confess to *WHAT*?"

"So that's the game you want to play, huh?" In a mad dash, Dazzlessence used his diamond edges to hack an entire row of jelly donuts apart. He returned to the table, covered in raspberry jam.

"*AHHHHH!* YOU MURDERED MY BABIES! THEIR BLOOD IS ON YOUR DIAMOND!"

"You jerk me around one more time and I destroy the entire farm!"

Doughy squeezed his lips together in defiance. Dazzlessence hacked up another row of the pastry farm. This time, he got the pomegranate turnovers.

"NOT THE TURNOVERS! STOP! STOP! PLEASE! STOP! FINE! I ADMIT IT!"

"Here then," Dazz said, sliding over his notebook and a pen. "Write out your confession."

Doughy scribbled as fast as he could. When he lifted the pen, Dazzlessence snatched the notebook back and read the confession aloud. "I, Doughy Bunington, confess to selling my signature apricot scone recipe on the moon black market."

What? Hanazuki thought.

"No, no, no, no, NO!" Dazzlessence ripped the confession from the notebook, crumpled it up, and threw it to the ground. "We want you to confess to chicknapping Tenders! You know, the MISSING CHICKEN PLANT BABY?"

Doughy lit up like a Christmas tree. "There's a missing Chicken Plant baby? Like, on the loose? Alone, vulnerable, and delicious? OH, HAPPY DAAAAAAY!"

"Not happy day! *NOT HAPPY AT ALL!*" Dazz sang angrily. "YOU CANNOT EAT THIS CHICKEN PLANT."

"How 'bout his wings?"

"NO."

Still, Doughy flapped his bun with excitement. "But did you know that Chicken Plants have wonderful regenerative abilities? That's why Chicken Plant was able to grow her wings back after I ate them. Regular chickens, not so much."

Hanazuki held Doughy's flapping bun in place. "How did you not know about Tenders?" she asked. "You're the one who made his cake, remember? It was in the shape of a chicken tender!"

"Silly me," Doughy said. "I'd thought you said, 'chai kin tender,' so I designed a cake that looked like a spilled cup of cardamom tea."

"Are you serious?"

"Let's pack it up," Dazzlessence said, slamming his notebook shut. "We've got to move on to the next suspect."

Hanazuki pulled Dazzlessence aside. "I'm worried that if left alone, Doughy will find Tenders before us."

Red was suddenly between them, jumping up and down with an idea, shouting, "ZA ZA ZA!"

That meant nothing to Hanazuki, so she plowed on. "What if he eats Tenders's wings, Dazz? Sure, they might grow back, but can you imagine the pain?"

Red shook his head, and his ears slapped against Hanazuki. "Seriously, Red? I've got ideas of my own, and I can't think straight!" Hanazuki held Red's ears still and watched Dazz sparkle with a plan.

"'Keep your friends close and your enemies closer,'" he said. "I read that on the back of a cereal box once."

"I like it. Make Doughy one of us."

"Exactly." Dazz approached Doughy, singing, with his hand out for a shake. "*Congratulations, you hotdog-meister! You are now promoted from serious suspect to . . .*"

Hanazuki joined him, and together they sang, "*Assistant detective!*"

"Me? Assistant detective?" Doughy squealed. "Leapin' linzer tortes!"

Red pointed to himself and shouted, "GRUH ZEE FROO GRA!"

"Sorry, Red," Hanazuki said. "The position is Doughy's."

"The position is *mine*," Doughy confirmed. Suddenly, his bun was styled like a trench coat and his crown was sitting on top of a fedora on his head.

"GAH-GAH ZEE GROO-ZEE ZAH!"

"I'm not *trying* to bruise your ego," Hanazuki explained to Red. "I'm just trying to keep Tenders safe."

“ZUH DUH ZOO.”

“This is about him, not you.”

“ZEEDER! MEE! ZEEDER MEE!”

“Fine! Tag along! If you want a real leadership role on the detective squad, you’re going to have to prove yourself. No complaining, no getting in the way. You have to be part of the team. OK?”

“PA GA,” Red shouted in agreement.

Hanazuki turned her attention to Dazz, who was studying his notebook. “*I need ideas and I need them now!*” he sang. “*Who’s got ’em? Shout ’em out to—*”

“Ahem,” Doughy cut in. He was sprawled across the picnic table, licking his lips. “More croissants, please.”

“You work for *us* now, Doughy,” Hanazuki snapped. “If you want brain fuel for the road, you’re going to have to grab it yourself.”

Doughy groaned and rolled off the table onto the bench and then to the moon earth. Then he waddled into the pastry farm and returned with eleven cronuts. "Speaking of brain fuel, have you talked to my mean brain neighbor? I've been waiting for the chance to interrogate him ever since he called me a rubbish bucket."

It was the first helpful thing Doughy had said all morning. Of *course* they should be questioning the maniacal brain in a cave! Hanazuki and Dazz smirked at each other, ready to rock. Next stop: Basal Ganglia.

CHAPTER FIVE

WHAT IS A CHICKEN BRAIN?

"Well, hello there, Hanakooki," Basal Ganglia said.

"It's Hanazuki," Hanazuki corrected him. "You know it's Hanazuki."

"Do I?"

"Yes. We've gone over it, like, a million times." Hanazuki exhaled, readying herself. It was interrogation time. "We've come to talk to you about something very important." She watched Basal Ganglia shift his eyes around his cave. Dazzlessence Jones was circling, writing in his notebook. Doughy Bunington was in the corner, eating a donut out of his fedora. Red Hemka had annoyingly climbed up onto Hanazuki's head. She had no idea why. For intimidation purposes? If so, it was unclear whether the intimidation was working or not.

"Did you know, Hazakooni, that repetition is good for the brain?" Basal asked.

"I did not know that," Hanazuki said.

"I know a lot of things, Hakazooni."

"Supercool! So. Here's the deal."

"Basal Ganglia the Great is closed for deals."

"I just meant that I'm going to tell you something."

"Not if I tell you something first. *MWAH HA HA HA!*" Basal laughed on and on and on and on and on and on and on and on and on and on and on.

This wasn't working. Hanazuki waved at Dazz for help, but his nose was buried in his notebook. She waved at Doughy instead. He waved back. "No, Doughy," she mouthed. "Help me."

"You got it!" Doughy pressed a donut to Basal's frontal lobes. "Assistant detective to the rescue!"

That wasn't exactly what Hanazuki had had in mind, but it seemed to have a positive impact. Red clapped his ears over his head, egging Doughy on. Doughy curtseyed.

Meanwhile, Basal asked, "What is this traitor of a pastry?" He squirmed to remove the flakes from his membrane. "Is it a *donut* or a *croissant*?"

"Both," Doughy replied, very much pleased with himself.

Basal shook his lobes, very much displeased. "Pick one, sausage-stinker. Donut or croissant. The pastry can only be *one* thing. It doesn't make sense. My cortex cannot compute it!"

"Uh, guys?" Hanazuki said. "We are MAJORLY off task here. We came here, Basal, to talk to you about Tenders. Do you know Tenders? He's a Chicken Plant. About yea high." Hanazuki held her hand down beside her knee.

"Ah, yes. Tenders," Basal said.

"He's been chicknapped," Hanazuki explained.

"Ah, yes. Chicknapped."

"Do you know *who* chicknapped him?"

"Ah, yes, Hanakoozi. I do."

"Who?!"

"ME! I DID IT! I'M THE RULER OF THE MOON. I WIN! ME! I CHICKNAPPED TENDERS! *MWAH HA HA HA HA HA HA HA HA HA HA HA!*"

Hanazuki wasn't sure if she should feel relieved

that they'd cracked the case or terrified that Basal Ganglia was behind the chicknapping. She focused on the relief and allowed herself to smile. The maniac brain in a cave was responsible! She could go back to Chicken Plant with some actual news! Progress had been made!

"Don't get too excited," Dazz whispered to her. "We still need to get Tenders back safe and sound."

"Copy that." It was time to push Basal to the next step. Hanazuki dropped back into serious detective mode and yelled over his laughter, which was laughier and crazier than ever. "SO, AS YOU CAN PROBABLY GUESS, WE'RE GOING TO NEED TENDERS BACK."

There was a long silence. "*Well, well, well,*" Basal finally said. "What do you know? The Moonflower with a red basket case on her head needs my help."

Red began to growl, and suddenly Hanazuki had a migraine.

"Actually, Red, can you get off?" she asked him. He hopped to the ground. "Tell us what you want, Basal."

"Well, as any half-wit might guess, I would like to be declared ROTMAPFAPCAFCBIAR."

"Which stands for?"

"'Ruler of the Moon and Pardoned for All Past Crimes and Future Crimes Because I Am Ruler.'"

Hanazuki glared at him. She was the one who was supposed to make the deals. Not the chicknapper! Still, what choice did she have? She clarified. "If I agree to whatever you just said, then you'll return Tenders safe and sound, right?"

"Maybe."

"What do you mean, 'Maybe'?"

"Exactly that. Maybe, baby."

Before Hanazuki could so much as scream, Dazzlessence threw down his notebook and sang, "*This diamond is taking the wheel!*" He got right in Basal's face. "Listen up, you smelly infected brain jam. Tenders is this moon's baby. Tenders is this moon's heart. Tenders is this moon's symbol of hope. What you have done has ripped this moon apart. Ruler, you say? Ha! Decent rulers don't CHICKNAP. Decent rulers don't say they're CLOSED FOR DEALS and then try to MAKE DEALS. Decent rulers don't DEMAND IMMUNITY and then *MAYBE* offer to GIVE BACK THE CHICKNAPPED CHICK PLANT IN RETURN!"

"Is that so?" Basal asked Dazzlessence, a smile playing on his lippy lobes. "So what *do* decent rulers do, you Wild Western overpriced jewel?"

"*The opposite of everything you dooooooooo!*"

"You go, Dazz!" Hanazuki cheered. "You tell him!"

"That's funny," Basal mused. "Do you suggest I follow *your* lead, Dazzy boy? Must I *sing* to get my way? Is that your recommendation for the moon's mastermind?"

"Don't diss my singing."

"You have an unpleasant vibrato," Basal said. "I have a pleasant vibrato. *La! La! Laaaaaaaaaaaaa!*" He sounded like a strangled cat. Hanazuki stuck her fingers in her ears.

"That's it," Dazz snarled. "Assistant Detective Doughy B, hand me another donut."

There was a menacing pause.

"Oh, me?" Doughy finally asked, now paying attention. "I'm all out."

Red offered Dazz the two cronuts he'd tucked away in his ears. Dazz took them and stormed toward Basal.

"NO, NO, NO! DON'T YOU DARE!"

"I don't like my pastries being used as punishment," Doughy muttered. "I find this very insulting."

Undeterred, Dazzlessence shoved the pastries into Basal's lobes.

Hanazuki's Moodblossom began to pulse red. She was feeling feisty and fiery!

"*Booyah*," Hanazuki said, snapping her fingers together with the flick of her wrist.

"SHU GRAH," Red shouted, snapping his ears together with the flick of his neck.

Dazzlessence put his diamond shoulder right up to Basal's cerebellum. "Now spill where Tenders is, or I'll really go diamond in the rough on you!"

"YOU HEAR THAT, YOU HORRIBLE SACK OF NEURONS?" Hanazuki shouted at Basal, her bracelet pulsing red, too. Red Hemka was excitedly gripping her neck, which was more than unpleasant, so she tossed him in the air. He morphed into a devil, then landed in her arms as his squishy self. Hanazuki didn't want Red in her arms, so she tossed him again. He morphed into a devil again. They did this on repeat—toss, devil, normal—until Red decided to shake things up and poke Basal with his ears.

"I wish you would stop, tomato bunny."

"Red, please," Hanazuki said, peeling him off of Basal. "I'm trying to do something here."

"Thank you," Basal said.

"I didn't stop Red for YOU!" Hanazuki shouted. "You are the EVILEST BRAIN in the MOONIVERSE! If you don't tell us where Tenders is RIGHT NOW, I'm going to tell the brains on all the other moons just how EVIL you are through ECNYWYWAPO, which stands for—"

"Elite Cerebral Network You Wish You Were a Part Of."

"That's right, Mister! *BOOM!*" Hanazuki was feeling so unstoppable, she bent her knees and hopped from foot to foot like a professional boxer. Ooh baby, was she strong! Ooh baby, was she powerful! Ooh baby, was she feisty! Blowing off steam felt *amazing*!

That is, until Basal Ganglia burst into giggles. "*MWAH HA HEE HA HA HA HEE!*" Then, all her strong, powerful, feisty feelings got sucked right out of her. "Um, what's so funny?" she asked self-consciously.

"First of all, you're out of cronuts!" He giggled

some more, his pitch climbing. "Second of all, you think Chicken Brain and all the other brains think I'm *NICE*? Well, nice brains finish LAST! Go ahead. Go on the Elite Cerebral Network You Wish You Were a Part Of. And if you have any trouble connecting—the cable guy keeps changing the password—then write a letter. We'll photocopy it, and Little Dreamer will deliver it around the galaxy to all the brains. Ask that unicorn friend of yours. He knows what's up. Alert the presses: I'M NASTY! *MWAH HA HA HO HA HO HA!*"

Chicken Brain? Hanazuki wondered, chills crawling up her neck. *A letter?*

Hanazuki and Dazzlessence looked at each other. This mission was far from over. Next stop: Sleepy Unicorn.

CHAPTER SIX

THE PLOT CHICKENS

"SLEEPY! SLEEPY! SLEEPY!" Underneath a giant purple mushroom, Hanazuki shook Sleepy Unicorn awake. "WE NEED YOUR HELP!"

"Well, hello, Hanazuki," Sleepy Unicorn drawled, mid-yawn. "Hello, Dazzlessence. Hello, Doughy. Hello, R—"

"Red, that's right," Hanazuki broke in. "Hi. Yes. We're all here. Hello."

Dazzlessence whipped his notebook out, ready for a confession. Doughy devoured a muffin top. Red held Sleepy by the mane. Hanazuki gripped Sleepy's shoulders and said, "We've got questions.

We need you to answer them honestly, and also super quickly."

"Wow. Sounds like a high-stakes job interview," Sleepy said, side-parting his mane. "Should I put on a tie? That might give me an advantage, looking profesh and all."

"No tie," Hanazuki said. "This isn't an interview."

In one fell swoop, Dazzlessence flipped Doughy's fedora off his head and onto his own. He sang, "Hold onto your hats—this is an *interrogation*!"

"I don't have hats," Sleepy said. "I don't even have one hat. Just pajamas. Wait, I'm not wearing pajamas. How embarrassing. Well, now you know. That's how I sleep."

"TMI," Dazz said. "Now, I'm only going to say this once, so listen good: We know about the 'Big L.'"

Sleepy touched his hooves to his heart. "*Love?*"

"What? No. The *letter*."

"Which one?" Sleepy asked. "'A' or 'B' or 'C'—"

"No, the *letter*, as in the *handwritten note*, as in the 'Dear *blah blah blah . . .*'"

“Blah Blah Blah?” Sleepy asked. “How confusing that someone should have the same first name and middle name and last name. Also, ‘Blah’

sounds like the name of a boring moon creature. Is he boring?"

Dazzlessence sang, "*AHHHH!*"

Hanazuki shouted, "*AGGGG!*"

Red yelled, "*YAAAA!*"

Doughy rubbed his bald head, just now realizing that his fedora and crown were missing.

Meanwhile, Sleepy had started to fall back asleep. In a fit of frustration, Red pinched him until his eyes were fully open. "We have a secret source who says you recently wrote a letter," Hanazuki said. "Did you or did you not write a letter?"

"Yes," Sleepy said.

"Yes, you did write a letter?" Hanazuki asked. "Or yes, you didn't?"

"No," Sleepy said.

"No, you didn't write a letter?" Hanazuki asked. "Or no, you did?"

"Both."

Red screamed.

"I wrote the letter with my hoof," Sleepy

explained, "but I didn't sign it from my hoof. I signed it from—*ZZZZZ.*" His legs sprawled out and he flopped to the ground. He was out again, snoring up a storm.

"Sleepy?" Hanazuki asked. She yanked his mane. Red pulled his ears. Dazz sang in his face, "*Sleepy? SLEEPY? SLEEEEEEEEEEEEEPY?!*"

Sleepy's eyes shot open. "Oh, hey there, Dazz. Oh, hey there—"

"Yup, we're all still here," Hanazuki cut in. "Who did you sign the letter from?"

"Tenders," Sleepy answered.

"Tenders!!!" Dazz exclaimed. "*We're on the right track, baaaaaby!*"

"The letter you wrote for Tenders," Hanazuki asked Sleepy. "Who was it addressed to?"

"I can't possibly remember *all* their names," Sleepy said.

"One," Hanazuki said. "Just remember one."

"Duck."

"A duck?"

"No, a chicken."

"How? Why?"

"So! Many! Questions!" Sleepy fanned himself with Red's ear. Red shape-shifted back into a devil. Sleepy screamed and released Red's ear, which was now a pitchfork.

"RED! ENOUGH WITH THE SHAPE-SHIFTING!" Hanazuki shouted. "YOU'RE LIKE A FIRECRACKER THAT CAN'T SIT STILL!"

"ZOO WHOA SHAW GUH MA BA DA PEY KEY REEEEE!" Red threw himself into the air, spun in a circle and then flung his ears wide like an exploding firecracker as he spun down on top of Sleepy's hair.

"SERIOUSLY?! Are you *TRYING* to stop me from doing my job?!"

"There's a lot of hot tempers in this 'shroom," Sleepy said warily. "I need to loosen my tie. Where's my tie?" He looked at Dazz. "Oh, right. You never gave me the chance to put it on. Can I borrow your hat?"

"*There's* my hat!" Doughy said. "I've been looking all over for it!"

"ZZZZZZZZZZZZZZ."

"SLEEPY!" Hanazuki shouted. She tickled under Sleepy's arms. Red jumped on his back. She tugged at his tail. Red whistled in his ears. Nothing. Sleepy was fast asleep.

"Should we call it?" Hanazuki asked, defeated.

"Onward and upward," Dazz said.

Just as the detective squad was about to leave, Sleepy's dream mystically appeared through a holographic projection: It was the tail end of Tenders's birthday party. It was late. The Chicken Dance was playing for the thirty-ninth time. Tenders waved Sleepy Unicorn over to him. Three power naps later, Sleepy made it across the dance floor and asked, "What's going on, Chicken Tenders?"

Tenders replied, "Unicuncle Sleepy, can you write a letter for me? I hear you're good at getting letters places because of your magic."

"I am, Little T. You tell me what you want it to say, and I'll write it for you. I've always wanted to be a scribe. Or a dentist. Anyway, I'll send the letter wherever you want through space spam."

"Space spam?"

"It's like snail mail, but without the snails. Whoever gets it will see a robotic version of your face and will hear you speaking the message."

"Cool!"

Tenders whispered into Sleepy's ear, and Sleepy wrote down everything he said. It read:

Dear Junior, Chicklet, Nuggets, Parmigiana, Burger, Drumstick, Salad, Skewer, and Duck,

Wassup? This is Tenders. I am your brother. I am a Chicken Plant, not chicks like you. I am going to visit Chicken Moon to meet you. See you soon, my brothers from the same mother. The same mother is Chicken Plant, in case you forgot. I can't wait.

Bock bock,

~~Sleepy~~ Oops, I mean Tenders

"There's such a thing as *Chicken Moon*?" Hanazuki wondered aloud.

"What is it? A moon full of chickens?" Dazz asked.

"I'd like to go to there," Doughy said.

"How would Tenders even get to Chicken Moon?" Hanazuki asked.

"No idea," Dazz said, "but we need to *get ahold of Tenders* before he *departs the moon*, if he's even capable of *departing the moon*."

"I'll happily depart the moon for chicken wings," Doughy offered. "I mean for Chicken Moon. To find Tenders, and not eat his wings. I wouldn't even bring BBQ sauce."

"No one's asking you to leave the moon," Hanazuki told him. "We just need Sleepy awake."

Red raised his ear like he was on it, but then all he did was slap the holographic projection.

"Uh, Red?" Hanazuki said. "That's not exactly gonna jolt Sleepy from his slumber."

She was right. All it did was jolt Sleepy to his

back with his legs up in the air. Then he began to snore louder than a Mazzadril with a sinus infection while the hologram disappeared.

"No, no, NO! Now what?!" Hanazuki asked. "We need to know what's going on."

"I CAN HELP!" Kiyoshi called out, suddenly running toward them with a bowl of black treasure fruit. He arrived, a heaving mess. "As soon as I found out that Tenders was missing, I went over to the three black Treasure Trees on your moon to read their fruit for clues as to where he might be. But from the first tree, I learned that one day, I'll need braces. From the second tree, I learned that Sleepy Unicorn was sleeping. Finally, from the third tree, I learned something relevant!"

"You could have skipped all that and gotten straight to the relevant part," Hanazuki said.

"Oh. Right," Kiyoshi said. "Well, I saw that Chicken Moon is where Chicken Plant's chicks go when they sprout a feather and float off into the galaxy. That's also where Chicken Brain lives. And also, that's where Tenders is now."

"Tenders is on Chicken Moon NOW?!" Hanazuki asked. "How'd he even get there?"

"Not sure, but I brought the fruit bowl for this very purpose. Hold on." Kiyoshi peered into the bowl of black treasure fruit. He gulped.

"Well?" Hanazuki pressed.

"Kiazuki," Kiyoshi croaked. "That's how Tenders got to Chicken Moon."

"Tell me EVERYTHING."

"OK, OK." He squinted at the fruit, gathering more clues. "Did you know that Chicken Plant was born on Chicken Moon?"

"She was? But she's rooted here!"

"Yeah, but apparently, she was first rooted on Chicken Moon. She was the first of her kind, and back then, Chicken Brain didn't know what to do with her. He thought she was a freak, so he sent her here." His eyes widened as he soaked up more clues from the fruit. "After that, there was a Chicken Plant Rights Revolution that was successful in giving Chicken Plants equal rights to unrooted chickens. Now Chicken Plants who are born on Chicken Moon are accepted and understood."

"That's beautiful," Doughy said, wiping a tear from his eye.

Kiyoshi kept his gaze on the fruit. "Even though Chicken Plants are rooted in the moon earth, they can be uprooted and re-rooted elsewhere, especially when they're young and their roots aren't so deep."

"*Hold uuuuup*," Dazzlessence sang. "So just like a youngster, Chicken Plant was uprooted from Chicken Moon and sent to Hanazuki's moon to be re-rooted, and Tenders was uprooted by Kiazuki and has probably been re-rooted on Chicken Moon, at least temporarily?"

Kiyoshi shrugged. "I think?"

"RA YA FLO FLY?" Red asked.

"Chicken plants can't float or fly like chickens,"

Kiyoshi told him, "but they can be carried by other chickens or travel by spacesurfer."

"So that's how she did it," Hanazuki said.

Kiyoshi half-nodded. "Yeah, I imagine Kiazuki took the spacesurfer to Chicken Moon."

Without so much as a beat, Hanazuki leaped through the closest Mouth Portal. "KIAZUKI, YOU'RE TOAST!"

CHAPTER SEVEN

CASE CRACKED

"THERE SHE IS!" Hanazuki pointed up at Kiazuki and Zikoro. They were hovering in their spacesurfer, trying to make a landing.

"Hanazuki, move," Kiazuki blared through the spacesurfer's speaker.

"GRUH GRAH ZOO," Red shouted back, just now arriving.

"Great," Hanazuki mumbled. Then to Kiazuki, "I'm not moving until I get an explanation."

"I can't explain anything from up here!"

"Then I guess we've got a problem!"

Kiazuki shifted the lever and landed twenty feet away, crushing four scraggly bushes. She and Zikoro hopped out of the spacesurfer and clawed their way to the parking spot. "What is your problem, Hanazuki?"

"What is *your problem*?" Hanazuki fired back. "You can't just *chicknap* Tenders and drop him off at another moon without his mother's permission!"

"Uh, *chicknap*?"

Red demonstrated by abducting Zikoro. He muffled Zikoro's screams by pressing his ear over his mouth and then dragged him behind a tree.

"Yes, I know the *definition* of chicknap, thank you very much," Kiazuki said. "Didn't you get my note?"

"What *note*?" Hanazuki asked.

"The note I left in Chicken Plant's nest."

"Um." Hanazuki felt her skin get clammy. She wasn't sure if she was nervous or annoyed or confused. Well, she was definitely confused. "Wait, go back."

"Ugh, why write a note if nobody reads the note?!" Kiazuki plopped down on a patch of moongrass. "I wasn't trying to be sketchy. I was trying to do the right thing."

"The right thing?"

"Yup. Just said that. Look, remember when during Tenders's birthday party you found me on the Dark Side of the Moon?"

"Yeah . . ."

"Well, I wasn't scheming with Basal Ganglia—you're right, he's crazy—but I did seek his counsel to help Tenders get in touch with his siblings. Turns out, they're all together on this bizarro moon called Chicken Moon. Basal knows all about it because he's in a fantasy moonball league with Chicken Brain. He gave me spacesurfer directions, and I just had to go."

"What's fantasy moonball?"

"That's literally the least important thing I just said." Kiazuki clapped at Red. "Mr. Feistypants, can you please release Zikoro?"

Red released him. They bowed as if it were the end of a performance.

"So, anyway," Kiazuki said, "I told Tenders to write a letter to his siblings. He got help from Sleepy, who space-spammed the thing off. Then I helped Tenders uproot."

"Let's talk about the uprooting part," Hanazuki said. "Was it painful?"

"I don't think so," Kiazuki said. "Tenders wrapped his wings around my neck, and I basically plucked him from the moon earth. I imagine it was like ripping off a Band-Aid. Hurts for a second, but then it's over." She leaned back on her elbows and crossed her legs. "Anyway, I left a note behind, and then we had a really nice ride over to Chicken Moon."

"I don't understand," Hanazuki said. "Why, Kiazuki? Why would you do any of this?"

Kiazuki took a moment, then picked at the moongrass. "Moon creatures can be misunderstood," she said softly. "Take Zikoro, for instance."

Hanazuki glanced at Zikoro. He was chasing

Red around a blue Treasure Tree, his fangs out. When he caught up to Red, he attacked him with slobbery kisses.

"Zikoro seems scary, but he's just annoying," Kiazuki said. "Also, he's separated from the rest of the Zikoros, and that's sad. I thought it would be nice for Tenders to meet his brothers and sisters. Maybe the tween chicks seem scary, but they're also *just* annoying."

"They're not *just* annoying," Hanazuki argued.

"Well, maybe since Tenders is so tender, he'll be a good role model for them."

"That, or they'll destroy him."

"UGH! Why are you being like this?!" Kiazuki tossed a fistful of moongrass at Hanazuki. "Look, Tenders deserves the chance to meet his siblings and form his own opinion about them. If he'd only *heard* about them, he'd be totally scared!"

"Kiazuki, he *should* be scared. We feel fear for a reason!"

"Oh, yeah? What's the reason?"

"The chicks are literal monsters."

"That's what you thought about Tenders, and look how he turned out!" Kiazuki stood, slapping the moongrass from her skirt. "Also, you're welcome. I just did Chicken Plant a huge favor."

"*Favor?*" Hanazuki repeated. "You took away her son!"

"*Psh*-yeah. News flash: She hates mothering. She's literally the *worst* mother. No way did she want another Chicken Plant rooted next to her for life!"

Hanazuki felt her head spin. "If you'd paid attention at the party, you'd know that Chicken Plant really did want Tenders by her side, but you were too busy 'not scheming' with Basal Ganglia!"

"OH, HEY-YO, LADIES," Maroshi greeted them, gliding toward them on his surfboard. "Look at us making waves."

"Not now, Maroshi," Kiazuki said.

"We're in the middle of something," Hanazuki said.

Maroshi kicked up his surfboard and ran a hand through his blue hair. "Yeaaaaah, you're gonna wanna hear this. It's kind of a big, brutal deal."

Kiazuki and Hanazuki looked at him with nervous anticipation.

"While I was off surfing the galaxy, I spotted a whole clutch of chickeroos—including Tenders—mad floating."

"*Mad* floating?" Hanazuki asked.

"The 'mad' part's just an expression. They could have been mad. Or chill. I was too far out to catch their temps. I just mean that they were hardcore floating."

"Hardcore floating where?" Hanazuki asked.

Maroshi licked the tip of his finger and held it up in the air. "Here."

In a panic, Hanazuki and Kiazuki looked up

at the sky. No chickens. Only Little Dreamer, dressed in a turkey onesie. He dropped a treasure shaped like a moon into Hanazuki's hands. She held it and it pulsed red.

"Well, that's ironic," Kiazuki joked.

"THIS ISN'T FUNNY, KIAZUKI!" Hanazuki shouted at her, getting up in her face. "Do you have ANY IDEA what you've done?!"

"What I'VE done?" Kiazuki shouted back. Their noses were practically rubbing. "I DIDN'T TELL THE CHICKS TO COME BACK!"

Red Hemka got between them, pushing Kiazuki away with one ear and Hanazuki away with the other. Then, when his ears stretched to capacity, a note that had apparently been tucked inside his ear slipped to the ground.

Hanazuki froze. "Don't tell me that's—"

"Yup," Kiazuki said. "I wasn't lying."

Hanazuki snatched the note from the ground and read it aloud:

Dear Chicken Plant,

Good-byes are rough, and you're a grouch. So, Tenders and I opted for the midnight steal to Chicken Moon. While he visits his brothers and sisters, we hope you'll appreciate the alone time. You're very welcome.

I luv u mama and moon friends!,

Kiazuki (+ Tenders)

Her insides on fire, Hanazuki stormed over to Red. "ARE YOU KIDDING ME? Did you *STEAL* Kiazuki's note from Chicken Plant's nest?!"

Red shook his ears, speechless.

"TELL THE TRUTH."

Red shrugged. He cocked his head. Then he flared his nostrils.

"You withheld evidence about Tenders's whereabouts this WHOLE TIME?" Her heart was pounding a million beats per second. "So. Did you *enjoy* messing things up every step of the way? Did you *want* to put Tenders's well-being in danger? Did you *have fun* worrying me sick trying to figure it all out when you had the answer in your *ear*?!"

Red narrowed his eyes. He bared his teeth. "BUH DUH GUH." He pointed at Hanazuki with his ears. Then at himself. He covered his face. He hopped up and down, and shouted, "BAH! BAH! BAH!"

Hanazuki looked up at the sky and tried to breathe. Maybe Red was trying to explain himself. Maybe he was just throwing a fit. She didn't care. She was too distracted by the floating clutch of tween chicks suddenly appearing in the distant sky. "You know what?" she said to Red. "Just stay away from me while I *actually* solve this problem."

Red let it rip. "BAAAAAAAAAAAAAH!"

Hanazuki stormed off, punching some low-riding marshmallow clouds. She was going to need an army to defeat the tween chicks, and she'd just lost her Moonflower sister to recklessness and Red to betrayal. Now what?

She was going to need a moon miracle.

CHAPTER EIGHT

THE CLUTCH IS ALL HERE!

"LINK UP, MOON CREATURES," Hanazuki commanded. "THIS IS WAR!"

Hanazuki, Dazzlessence Jones, Sleepy Unicorn, Doughy Bunington, nine Hemka, Kiyoshi, Maroshi, and Chicken Plant fixed themselves in a line—arms, ears, and wings linked—in defense against the tween clutch of chicks floating menacingly toward them.

"*PUT YOUR WINGS UP*," Dazzlessence sang up at them.

"*Bock, bock, bock, bock?*" they bocked in reply.

"*I REPEAT*," Dazz sang, flashing his badge, "*PUT YOUR WINGS UP*."

They obeyed. But now that their wings were

pulled in, they could no longer float. They dropped through the galaxy, full-speed, and landed on the moon earth—*thud, thud, thud, thud, thud, thud, thud, thud, thud, thud!*—a ten-chick pileup.

Hanazuki stepped forward. "If this is a CHICKEN COUP, we will NOT STAND FOR IT."

"Do you mean a chicken *coop*?" a funky-looking but familiar chick asked, sticking his head out from the middle of the chicken pile.

An athletic-looking chick wearing shin guards stood at the top of the pile like an Olympian. "Coops are great for team sports," he said, stretching a wing across his chest.

"Huh?" Hanazuki said. "No, not a *coop*. A *coup*."

"Doves coo," said a nerdy chick with horn-rimmed glasses held together at the bridge of his nose with tape. "They take a gulp of air, their chest expands, and the haunting sound comes out their nostrils!"

"I can make a haunting sound," said an emo chick with a feather swooped over his right eye. *"LooLooLooLooLooLooLooLooLooLooLoo LooLooLooLooLooLooLooLooLoo."*

Hanazuki eyed the chicks with suspicion. They were so cute! And silly! And weird! Was it all a front? Were they trying to melt her heart? Soften her army? So that they could destroy the moon? What was going on?!

"ENOUGH," Hanazuki finally said, curtailing the emo chick's birdcall. "I see right through you. I SEE RIGHT THROUGH ALL OF YOU!"

The chicks looked down at their bellies, trying to see through their feathers.

"Um, not literally," Hanazuki clarified. She turned to the emo chick. "Explain that birdcall. A message to your army back home?"

"We don't have armies," said a hippie chick. "We have wingies."

"Because we don't have arms," explained a tiny chick. "We have wings."

"*OK*," Hanazuki said. The chicks were climbing out from the pile, clapping the moon dust from their feathers, hugging each other, and feeding on dried worms from bags. There was, seemingly, not a bad bone in their bodies, except for the bad boy chick in a leather jacket. Well, if he weren't sporting an EQUAL CHICKEN RIGHTS pin, and sharing his worms, and also sharing his jacket. *Ahhhh!* Even the bad boy chick was *good!* How was she supposed to stand up to their cuteness?!

Hanazuki looked back at the line of moon creatures to get their take on all of this, but they'd disbanded. They were in a clump, sighing and smiling at the chicks as if they were the stars of the most adorable zoo exhibit in the mooniverse. *Everybody's gone soft*, Hanazuki worried. She would have to act alone. "Good afternoon, chicks of Chicken Moon," she said with as much authority as she could muster. "I am Hanazuki, the protector of this moon."

"Good afternoon, Hanazuki," the chicks chirped in unison.

With such obedience, they just had to be trying to throw her off, but thrown she would not be! "YOU SHALL NOT DESTROY MY MOON!" she shouted at them.

The chicks just stared at her.

"Hello?" Hanazuki said, prompting them to respond.

"Hello, I'm Salad," said the nerdy chick.

"I'm Burger," said the sporty chick.

"I'm Chicklet," said the tiny chick.

"I'm Nuggets," said a pudgy chick.

"I'm Parmigiana," said a feather-gelled chick.

"I'm Drumstick," said the hippie chick.

"I'm Skewer," said the bad boy chick.

"I'm Duck," said the emo chick.

"And I'm Junior," said the funky, familiar chick. "Hello."

Hanazuki gasped. "Junior as in *Junior*, the chick who scared off a Mazzadril?"

"That's me," he said, smiling with an overbite so overbitten, his bottom beak and top beak were entirely crossed.

Hanazuki's heart began to melt. She threw her arms around his neck. "I've missed you so much! Look at how much you've grown!"

"Thank you," said Junior.

"OH MY MOON GODS," Chicken Plant squawked from behind the huddle of moon creatures. "WHAT ABOUT TENDERS? REMEMBER HIM? MY CHICK PLANT WHO WAS CHICKNAPPED? FOCUS, H."

"Who's that?" Junior asked, pushing his neck out to see around Hanazuki.

"Nochicken," Hanazuki lied. She couldn't distract the chicks now. "Listen up, birdies. First order of business: Release Tenders. If you do as I say, no chick will get hurt."

"Hurt?" asked Chicklet, shrinking from the size of a chestnut to a peanut.

"Sorry, that's not—" Hanazuki cut herself off. "Obviously no chick is getting hurt. I just mean that if Tenders isn't released, there will be *trouble*."

"I like trouble," said Skewer, popping the collar of his leather jacket.

"Fine, then the opposite," Hanazuki said. "If Tenders isn't released, there will be *no trouble*."

"I prefer no trouble," said Salad. "I like a clean record."

"*That'a chick*," Dazz sang.

"Peace, love, freedom, now!" cheered Drumstick, setting fire to his Grateful Egg boxers. "Smell no, we won't go!"

Hanazuki blew a whistle dangling from her neck, cuing the Hemka. They extinguished the burning boxers with a bucket of goop. "HEY!" she shouted at the chicks. "NO SMELLY UNDERWEAR SACRIFICES. NO MORE COMPROMISES. HAND OVER TENDERS. NOW!"

"SURPRIIIIIIISE!" From the middle of the huddle of chicks, Tenders popped up, tossing a wingful of dried worms in the air like confetti. "It's me! Tenders! I'm back and ready to snack!"

Chicken Plant went ballistic, screaming, "MY SON! *Squawk*. MY TENDERS! *Squawk*. TENDERS, MY SON!"

"Mama?" Tenders asked, his eyes filling with tears. "Mama, I missed you!"

"*That's* Mama?" Junior asked, tossing Tenders on his back and pushing his way through the moon creatures toward her. The rest of the chicks followed, shoving and flapping with excitement. They circled her and serenaded her, *"Mama, mama, maaaaaama! It's been so long! We've grown so strong! We've missed everything about you! Mama is our mama. Mama, mama, maaaaaama! We are home!"*

"Who taught you to sing?" Chicken Plant asked, cringing. "That chick needs to be checked."

"Chicken Brain," answered Salad.

"*Him?*" Chicken Plant said. "Oh, most definitely checked."

"You're so funny! Mamma mia!" said Parmigiana, going in for a peck on each cheek.

"Mama, watch," said Chicklet the tiny chick. He somersaulted, then lifted his wings in the air for a grand finish. "Did you see me? Did you?"

"Your dirt bath? Unfortunately, yes."

"Now watch this," said Burger, doing a back wingspring.

"Mildly impressive," Chicken Plant said.

"Mama, do you like tie-dye?" asked Drumstick, holding out a bandana. "I made you this headband."

"Headwear makes my feathers flat."

"Tie-dye her a sock," suggested Nuggets.

"I don't have feet," Chicken Plant said.

"Exactly," said Duck.

The sighing, smiling moon creatures began to laugh. Hanazuki began to laugh, too. The chicks really were so cute! And silly! And weird! It wasn't a front! They were true heart-melters, army-softeners, distractors here to—*Um . . . wait*. What *were* they here for?

Hanazuki called out, "If you hear me, clap once." Some chicks clapped their wings. It sounded like rustling feathers. It was good enough. "So, chicks who clearly come in peace—"

"Peace NOW, freedom NOW!" chanted Drumstick.

"Yup, that's a peace chant," Hanazuki said, and then got back to it. "Chicks, please explain why you have journeyed all the way here."

Junior, who seemed to be the chick in charge, raised his wing.

"Yes, Junior," Hanazuki said, calling on him.

"When Tenders came to Chicken Moon, he described Mama so differently from how we all remembered her—"

"What's *that* supposed to mean?" Chicken Plant squawked, her wings on her hips.

"Oh, n-n-nothing," Junior stuttered. "I just mean that us chicks only spent the first few minutes of our lives on your moon, and so our memories are sorta fuzzy. It's hard for us to remember much of anything—we're chickens!—let alone the earliest moments of our lives!"

"Apology half-accepted. Good effort."

"Anyway," Junior said, "us chicks thought it would be a grand idea to visit."

"So that's why you're here?" Hanazuki asked. "To visit?"

"That," Junior said, "and to bring Mama back with us to Chicken Moon."

The chicks erupted in cheers. *"WE WANT A MAMA CHICK! WE WANT A MAMA CHICK!"*

Stressed and overwhelmed, Chicken Plant looked like she might snap from her stalk.

Hanazuki yelled over the chicks, "THAT'S SWEET, BUT YOU CAN'T JUST *TAKE* CHICKEN PLANT BACK WITH YOU! YOU KNOW THAT, RIGHT?"

Junior cut the chanting with a swoosh of his wing and asked, "Why not? Tenders came to Chicken Moon, and he's a Chick Plant."

"Exactly," Hanazuki said. "Tenders is a *Chick Plant*. Not a *Chicken Plant*. Chicken Plant's roots are deep in the moon earth. We can't just uproot her!"

Tenders coiled his roots like a phone charger and tucked them in his wing. "What do *you* think about all this, Mama?"

Chicken Plant's eyes welled up. "No thanks. I'm good."

"But you're crying," Tenders said.

"I'm not crying. YOU'RE crying."

"Of course I'm crying. I want you to come be our mother and you said no."

"Hold up," Chicken Plant said. "You're going back with them? You're leaving me AGAIN?"

"I have to. Chicken Moon is where I belong." Tenders swept his wing at his chick bros, and they nodded in agreement. "It's where you belong, too, Mama."

By now, Chicken Plant was sobbing. "Hey, you heard Hanazuki. My roots! Whaddya want from me?" She feathered her face. "'Chicken Moon is where I belong!' *Blech!* That's a bunch of bologna!"

"Bologna is right." Suddenly, Kiazuki was on

the scene. She and Red Hemka broke through the circle of moon creatures to the circle of chicks. "Hi, there!" she greeted them. "I'm Kiazuki. I saw you all from a distance when I dropped off Tenders. Good to see you again."

They chick-sandwiched her with a hug.

"Wow! See?" Kiazuki said to Hanazuki, amazed. "These chicks aren't demons! They're totally misunderstood! My plan was brilliant. You're welcome."

"*Maybe*," Hanazuki said.

"Maybe *what*? Look at Tenders. Look at how happy he is. He's practically exploding with joy."

"I think that's snot." Hanazuki wiped it away with the bottom of her skirt. "Anyway, the chicks want to bring Chicken Plant back with them to Chicken Moon, but that's really hard. Maybe impossible. She's way too rooted."

"OK, so someone else can go in her place."

"Like who?"

Kiazuki rolled her eyes. "Here we go again. This

isn't my moon. I shouldn't have to solve EVERY problem that floats your way."

"Wait," Hanazuki said, suddenly struck with the moon's most incredible idea. "What if . . . what if *you* went to Chicken Moon to be the chicks' mother? It would be temporary—a day or two max! They'd get a taste of motherhood, and you'd get a taste for caring for a healthy moon of your own!"

Kiazuki gave her a blank stare.

"Is that a yes?" Hanazuki asked.

"That's a no," Kiazuki said. "These little guys are sweet and all, but I'm feeling burnt out on the good deeds. I do so many of them. One after another after another after—"

"*Do* you, though?"

"I'm gonna sit this one out, thanks." Kiazuki started to walk away, but the chicks were dead set on Hanazuki's plan. Chanting over and over, "*MOTHER KIAZUKI! MOTHER KIAZUKI! AT LAST WE HAVE A MOTHER,*" they lifted and tossed her in the air! (Well, two inches tops. Even

Burger, the most athletic of the chicks, was only a foot tall.)

"Um, I already said no!" Kiazuki said. "Let me down!"

Then, out of nowhere, Red Hemka started shouting at the top of his feisty lungs, "BEE BAH! ZAH-ZAH! ME ME!"

The chicks lowered Kiazuki to the ground and gave Red their attention. Everyone did. He was so loud it was hard not to.

"ME MA! ME MA! GRUH-ZUH NO! ME YAH! ME MA!"

"Let me get this straight," Hanazuki said. "*You* want to go to Chicken Moon to be the chicks' mother?"

He nodded. "YA! YA! YOO YA! MA! MA MA!"

Hanazuki sighed. "C'mon, Red. There's no way I can put you in charge of anyone, let alone these chicks. Don't you remember? You put Tenders in danger!"

"DANJUH NO."

"Well, what *could have been* danger," Hanazuki clarified. "You didn't know what you were getting yourself into when you stole Kiazuki's note."

ME MA! ME MA! ME MA!"

"No," Hanazuki said firmly. "You can't go to Chicken Moon, and that's final."

"ME MA NO WEYE?"

"Because you betrayed me!"

"BAAAAAAAAAAAAAAAAAAAH!"

Hanazuki's Moodblossom started pulsing red. She spotted Little Dreamer zigzagging above her and dug into her pocket for his gifted treasures. She wanted to throw them all! Hard! But just when she had the treasures in her fist, ready to fire, she heard Chicken Plant screech, "FINE. I'LL GO. I'LL GO BACK TO CHICKEN MOON."

Hanazuki did a double take, her frustration dissolving to confusion. "But—but—what about your deep roots?"

"Oh, please," Chicken Plant said. "Don't be so dramatic. My roots are here, but way back when, they were on Chicken Moon. It's time I return for a visit. It's time I make Chicken Brain feel like a real Chicken Brain for getting rid of me. It's time I show every chicken the face of the Chicken Plants Rights Revolution 2.0!"

"Well, wow!" Hanazuki said. "I'm super proud of you. This is—this is GREAT!"

"Uproot me already. Just keep my stalk and body intact."

The chicks began freaking out with excitement, chanting, *"BOCK! BOCK! BOCK! BOCK! MAMA CHICKEN PLANT IS RETURNING! IT'S BEEN SO LONG! WE'VE GROWN SO STRONG! MAMA, MAMA, MAAAAAAMA IS COMING HOME!"* They swarmed her, trying to lift her from the moon earth.

"I said 'intact,' chickbrains," Chicken Plant said. "You break mama from her stalk and the deal's off the nest."

The chicks stopped pulling. Instead, they petted

her. Though gentle and compassionate, it was largely ineffective.

"All right, all right, step back, chicks," Dazzlessence sang, flashing his badge again—this time with more confidence. "Hey, *Sleeeeeepy*, are you up?" He paused, staring at Sleepy Unicorn lying on his belly, his eyes closed and his mouth drooling. "*Sleepy*?" Nothing. *"SLEEPY, WAKE UP NOW!"*

"Good morning," Sleepy said, his eyes fluttering open. "Or is it evening?"

"Don't matter." Dazzlessence swung his arm around Sleepy's shoulders. "Do you think you can unroot Chicken Plant with your magic?"

"Root veggies."

"No. *Unroot* Chicken Plant."

"Yams and yucca."

"Huh?"

"ZZZZZZ."

"NOOOOOOOO!" Dazz shook Sleepy Unicorn

awake and positioned him in front of Chicken Plant. "Stay with me, brother. Aim here—where the roots are under the moon earth—and *FIRE THAT LIGHTNING MAGIC!"*

"OK, I'll try my best." Sleepy aimed at the roots and fired, blowing up dust and exposing one wiry root.

"One root down, a thousand to go!" Dazz sang.

Chicken Plant squawked her head off. "STOP! YOU WANT MY FEATHERS TO CATCH ON FIRE? IS THAT WHAT YOU ALL *WANT*?"

Mortified, the chicks shook their heads.

"Can I go back to sleep now?" Sleepy asked.

"Um, hold on."

"ZZZZZZZ."

Enough is enough, Hanazuki thought. She went to throw down her red-pulsing treasures, but Red snagged them and hopped off. *No, he didn't!* Her blood began to boil. "HEY! RED! COME BACK RIGHT THIS INSTANT WITH *MY* TREASURES!"

Red stopped to juggle the three treasures.

Hanazuki caught up to him. She went to swipe the treasures from the air, but Red was too fast. He clutched them against his belly and hopped away on top of the chicks' heads, using them like river stones.

"Bock! Bock! Bock! Bock!" they bocked.

"You don't get to steal the note AND steal my treasures," Hanazuki huffed, sprinting after Red. He stopped, then dangled the treasures above the moon earth right beside Chicken Plant. "DON'T YOU DARE, RED! YOU KNOW THAT'S A TERRIBLE PLACE FOR TREES."

Hanazuki threw herself at Red, but it was too late. He dropped the treasures so close to Chicken Plant that they were touching the edge of her nest.

"Well, this is gonna be a wild ride," Chicken Plant said dryly. Just then, three big beautiful feisty red Treasure Trees sprouted around her, ramming her roots out from beneath the moon earth. She wavered back and forth until her stalk uprooted. Then, she fell into the feathery wings of her chicks. "Well, that worked."

While the chicks celebrated and readied Chicken Plant for travel, Hanazuki walked up to Red, blinking in shock. "Wait. Did you do that on purpose?"

Red nodded.

"Like you weren't trying to be annoying, just trying to help?"

Red nodded again, then threw his ears up. "FYE LEE!"

"Finally what?" Hanazuki asked.

"GRUH GREE SO JUH JAH MEEEEEE!"

"No way. You were trying to help me the *whole* time?"

Red nodded like crazy.

It was hard for Hanazuki to believe. She would have known if Red were trying to *help*, right? She took a deep, confused breath, and moments from the last several hours flashed through her head: Red charading. Red retrieving donuts for Doughy. Red morphing into a devil to scare Basal. Red slapping Sleepy Unicorn's holograph projection to jolt him awake. And now this. Planting feisty red Treasure Trees to help uproot Chicken Plant.

"Red," Hanazuki said softly, a wave of guilt rippling through her body. "I—I was being such a jerk." She wanted to cry, thinking about it all. How could she have been so blind? Red was suddenly by her side, squeezing her with love. Before she knew it, tears were rolling down her face, and an apology was flying out from her mouth. "I'm sorry I doubted your intentions. I'm sorry I kept brushing you off. I'm sorry I didn't acknowledge you as part of the detective squad!"

Red hugged her tighter. "ZEE ZOOBOO!"

Hanazuki rubbed her eyes dry. "I'm glad you're not going all the way to Chicken Moon. Even if you do annoy me sometimes. Or, like, a lot of times. I'd miss you too much." She paused, then scrunched her face, suddenly puzzled. "Hold up. I still don't get why you stole the note. What was that all about?"

Red's ears fell to the ground. "ME LUV. YU LUV. ME HAZZAH. ME! ME!"

"Because you love me? Because you wanted to spend more time with me?"

He stood tall and mimed placing a badge of honor around his neck, then tapped her wrist.

Suddenly, his charades were clear as day. "Because you wanted to show me what a good leader you are. Because you thought if the Tenders mystery stayed a mystery, then you'd have more time to prove yourself."

Red nodded slowly.

"But prove yourself how?"

"CHEE CHA REED ZU LEE." He shaded his eyes like he was searching for something. "NO MA HEE NAH." He pointed to Hanazuki, then to himself. "SUXEE DAT GETH ER."

Hanazuki translated. "You didn't know what the note said—you couldn't read it—and you didn't want to ask for *my help*. You wanted to *help me* crack the case. You weren't trying to make me fail. You were trying to make me succeed, and you hoped that we'd succeed *together*."

Red smiled.

"Wow—I'm impressed I got all that!" She laughed. "Well, just so you know, I admire your leadership. Even if it does lead to trouble. Trouble keeps things interesting!"

"Truth," Kiazuki said.

"'Interesting,'" Junior said. "Like the way I look."

"Sure!" Hanazuki glanced at the chicks. Their wings were spread and they were readying Chicken Plant for flight. "I'll miss you, CP," Hanazuki told her, laying a kiss on her cheek.

Chicken Plant pecked at her, but not in the kiss way. "What do you gotta miss me for?" she retorted. "I'll mama the chick out of these guys for a week, two weeks max. Then I'll be back."

The chicks giggled.

"Was that funny? It wasn't supposed to be." Chicken Plant raised a wing. "Let me just make one more thing clear. This isn't me embracing motherhood. This is a revenge trip." She looked at her chicks looking at her, and her voice cracked. "Sort of a revenge trip. Because you're my kids, and you don't live on the same planet as me. Not that I care. I mean, I'm angry at Chicken Brain, duh. The whole situation's unfair. And that's what I'm rising up against. Unfairness!" She flapped her wings, flustered. "OK, what are we waiting for? LET'S GO, CHICKS!"

The chicks kissed and hugged and flapped each other on the back. They didn't seem to care what Chicken Plant said she was going back for. They knew it was for them, and no matter what, she would always be their mama.

All of the chicks gathered around Chicken Plant and Tenders, ready to help them fly off the moon.

"ONE, TWO, THREE, FLY!" Junior and Tenders said together, and then, *whoosh*, with a flap of their wings, they were all floating off into the galaxy.

CHAPTER NINE

A MAMA HEN AND HER DENLESS DEN

This spot is perfect!" Hanazuki said, holding Chicken Plant's stalk above a shaded yet spacious plot of moon earth.

"I agree," Sleepy said. "There are no red Treasure Trees popping her personal bubble, but they're also not too far in case she gets hungry for fruit."

"GROO FROO ZEE-FOO," said Red Hemka, waving Hanazuki to the left.

"What do you think, Chicken Plant?" Hanazuki asked, following Red's instructions. "A little to the left? A little to the right? More in the shade? Farther from the tree?"

"Oh, my moon god. Just root me already."

"Will do." Hanazuki and Red Hemka untangled Chicken Plant's roots and fanned them out around the base of her stalk.

"You ready for me?" Sleepy asked. He pointed his horn at the roots and scrunched his face in concentration. "Four gulps of yellow goop, and I'm feeling *en-er-gized*!"

"That's great," Hanazuki said. "We definitely need lots of your energy. Chicken Plant, are *you* ready?"

"Too much talking. Not enough doing."

Hanazuki pointed at Sleepy. "ONE, TWO, FIRE AWAY!"

Sleepy Unicorn fired at the roots, and they twisted into the moon earth. One at a time. Super slowly. Chicken Plant squawked, "OW! YOW! FASTER! ENERGIZED MY BUM, YOU NAP

ADDICT! ZAP ME HARDER!" But this was as fast, as hard, and as energized as Sleepy could go.

Five screaming minutes later, Chicken Plant's roots were securely screwed into the ground. Red had shoveled dirt back over the roots, while Sleepy had collapsed beside him, fast asleep.

"Yay! Great work, team!" Hanazuki cheered.

Red clapped himself on the back. Sleepy let out a snore. Chicken Plant huffed. "Do I look like a mushroom to you, Unicorn?" Then she turned to Hanazuki. "This will not be his new sleeping quarters."

"Copy that." Hanazuki sat down beside Chicken Plant and stared up at her chicks, slowly making their way through the galaxy. All ten chicks had delivered their mama back to her moon, and now all ten were returning to Chicken Moon, mama-free.

Hanazuki glanced at Chicken Plant. Her chin was quivering. "So," Hanazuki began gently. "Wanna talk about it?"

"About what?" Chicken Plant asked.

"Chicken Moon?"

"Oh. *That.*" Chicken Plant exhaled. "It was exhausting. What a clutch of pains!"

"What do you mean? What happened?"

"Well, for starters, Tenders wanted to be rooted even closer to me than he was before. Junior wanted braces for his overbite. Chicklet wanted growth hormones. Burger had me enroll him in a hockey league. Parmigiana wanted pasta-making classes. Salad wanted contacts. Drumstick led drum circles right next to me. Skewer tattooed 'I heart Mama' on his neck, and then had the nerve to ask me to apply ointment to it twice a day. Duck stole Drumstick's tie-dye kit and bleached his feathers pink!" She sighed, throwing her wings up. "Can you believe my luck? How is it that I birthed such a high-maintenance clutch of fools?"

"I dunno," Hanazuki said. "I mean, *high-maintenance*? Where could they have possibly gotten that from?"

"Beats me."

Hanazuki laughed. "How was your revenge? Did Chicken Brain learn his lesson?"

"Don't get me started. I was so consumed with my chicks, I didn't even have the chance to give him a piece of my mind! Next time."

"So, there's a *next time*?"

"Duh. It would be irresponsible for me to stay here forever. Chicken Plant rights are a major issue. The chickens and Chicken Plants of Chicken Moon have a right to know their history. *I* am their history!"

"That makes sense." Hanazuki nudged her playfully. "But I bet it'll also be nice to see Tenders and the rest of your chicks again, right?"

"Oh, you think I'd go all the way back to Chicken Moon for *THEM*? I just told you what PAINS they were. WERE YOU EVEN LISTENING?!"

Hanazuki shrugged. "Hey, you are a mama after all."

"What's *that* supposed to mean?"

"Going nuts, getting gruff, feeling feisty—it's all part of the experience."

Just then, Little Dreamer flew down and dropped Hanazuki a treasure shaped like a smiling Hemka. "*Awwww!* Thanks, snoozy dude. This is the cutest treasure you've ever given me!"

"Shee-la-la."

"Totally, though the chicken treasure was pretty cute, too. Right, CP?"

"Please don't," Chicken Plant said.

Hanazuki giggled, then kissed the top of Red's head. He wiped her red fruit lip stain away, then hugged her back.

"Well, I'm looking forward to a nice, long, peaceful nap," Chicken Plant said. "I'm an empty nester now, and I'm gonna live my full empty-nester life."

"Sounds like a plan well-deserved."

Chicken Plant closed her eyes, and Hanazuki took Red's ear in her hand and began to walk away, but after only a few steps they were stopped in their tracks by Chicken Plant's scream. It was so loud the red Treasure Trees started bending. It was so loud their fruit started dropping. It was so loud that Sleepy Unicorn *almost* woke up!

"*AHHHH!*" Chicken Plant cried. "Help! Egg! Inside! Coming out! *HEEEEEELP!*"

Hanazuki's heart began to flutter. *Here we go again*. She and Red stared at Chicken Plant as she popped another egg out. It dropped to her nest, quaking. And then it started to hatch . . .

Hanazuki and her moon crew are always up for an out-of-this-world adventure! Don't miss a single one!

Available wherever books are sold.
Also available as an ebook.

Text by Stacy Davidowitz. Illustrations by Victoria Ying.
Published in 2018 by Amulet Books, an imprint of ABRAMS.

CHAPTER ONE

OF CHAOS AND COMETS

Clack, clack, clack! Hanazuki abruptly awoke to the clapping of moon rocks. She opened her eyes, and bouncing in a frenzy were her ten squishy friends, the Hemka. "Is there a snooze option around here?" she asked, exploding into a Moonflower yawn.

"Ya, ya, ya, yee-yoo," they replied.

"OK, great, clap me up in five."

Just as Hanazuki collapsed back into her sleeping bag, Red Hemka and Yellow Hemka pulled her out by her arms. Blue Hemka clung to her left leg. Pink Hemka clung to her right leg. Lavender Hemka screamed, "YEEEEEEE!" into her left ear. Teal Hemka screamed, "YOOOOOOO!" into her right ear. Orange Hemka, Green Hemka, and Purple Hemka stared at her like nervous spaceballs.

"And . . . I'm up! At the crack of moon! One of you please explain why you're all freaking out!"

Lime Green Hemka leaped into her lap, cowered in the crook of her armpit, and answered, "YA-YA-YEE-YEE-YOO-YOO-YAAAAA!"

"Aw, Lime Green, did you have a nightmare?"

He shook his head.

"A morningmare?"

Another no.

Hanazuki smiled and tickled him until he shouted, "Ya-ya-ya-ya-ya!" which sounded like laughter but was actually just the noise he made when he was having a panic attack.

"Well, whatever woke you all up—it wasn't a *real*mare. There's nothing to be afraid of. Look around!" Hanazuki swept her arm across the beautiful moon. To her left was the Rainbow Swirl Lake. To her right was a garden of Treasure

Trees. Up above were floating marshmallow clouds. "We are on the Light Side of the Moon, aka the *bright side* of the moon, remember? Here the rainbow waterfalls sparkle, and the Treasure Trees protect us, and there's no reason to be hiding in my armpit. Deep breaths!"

Lime Green stuck his head out from underneath Hanazuki's armpit and began to wheeze.

"That doesn't sound promising. Hold on." Hanazuki quickly gathered two giant Treasure Tree leaves and glued their edges together with goop. "Voila! It's a breathing bag! Breathe in and the leaves press together; breathe out and it blows up like a balloon. Helps steady your breath."

Hanazuki tried to pass the breathing bag to Lime Green, but Orange Hemka snatched it away.

"Very funny, Orange. Always a fan of your wackiness, but—"

Orange hopped away, the breathing bag clutched between his floppy ears.

"Oh, come on, Orange! It's way too early for running!"

Hanazuki leaped from her sleeping nook with Lime Green on her back and attempted to chase Orange down. They ran past a sleeping Talking Pyramid.

"Morning, Hana Z," he blurted, startled awake. "With the new day comes fresh problems, I see."

"Yup!" Hanazuki shouted behind her. "A small dose of morning chaos, though, usually makes for a chill-tastic afternoon."

"The storm before the calm."

"Ha, exactly!"

Orange slid down a crater, entering the moon's most lush and colorful Treasure Tree garden. Hanazuki followed. When she was finally at Orange's heels, he stopped short. Hanazuki crashed into him, and the breathing bag flew from his ears, catching on a red Treasure Tree branch totally out of reach. "Oh, moonshakes!"

she cried, then shook a fist at Orange. "Now see what you've done!"

Lime Green slid from Hanazuki's back and practically melted to the ground.

"Orange, why in the moon would you steal Lime Green's breathing bag?" she asked. "Don't you want to help? He's majorly freaked out. Over, um, *something*."

"Yoo-gee-yee!" Orange screeched, pointing his ears up to the bag.

"Yup, that's the bag."

"Yoo-gee-yee-cha," Orange screeched louder.

"Yup, it's stuck."

By now all the Hemka had arrived at the crime scene and were pointing their ears at the bag, too. What was this—early morning recess?! "Not. A. Toy," Hanazuki told them. "But hey, if you all want to play with the bag, then why don't you shapeshift into a ladder and grab it yourselves? You guys *do* shapeshift, right?"

All of a sudden, the red Treasure Tree let out a low, rumbling "*Mmmooooaaan.*"

"Oh, no! What's wrong?" Hanazuki asked the tree, laying a gentle hand on its trembling trunk. The breathing bag was shaken free. It floated onto Lime Green's head. He did nothing but wear it as a hat.

"Buddy, use it," Hanazuki urged. "I *did not* just chase down Orange for nothing." But Lime Green didn't use the bag. He sat as still as a moon rock, his eyes halfway out of their sockets, looking at the branch where the breathing bag had just been. Same with the other Hemka. They couldn't keep their eyes from the shaking tree.

Just as Hanazuki began to follow their gaze, a treasure fruit smacked her on the forehead and knocked her flat on her back. "OW! What the—?" Red fruit of all sizes began dropping from the tree's branches onto her body. *Plop! Plop! Plop!* Before she could investigate the tree's health—Treasure Trees don't just shed their fruit!—she was buried under a fruit-salad avalanche.

Once the fruit stopped falling, Hanazuki shook her head and the treasure berries fell from her eyes. Through the barren branches she could see the sky, and in it were two fiery comets! They were about to collide! Dangerously close to her moon! *So* that's *why Lime Green was freaking out! That's why all the Hemka were freaking out!* "That's real. That's really real. And bad. Really, really real and bad."

Lime Green wriggled his way through the fruit to get back beneath her armpit. "Yo-yo-*yee-yee*," *he* whimpered.

Hanazuki's heart pounded with the fervor of a zillion exploding stars. A puddle of nerves, she couldn't move. "Do something," she uttered, trying to get herself to take action.

But Lime Green must have thought Hanazuki was insisting that *he* do something, since he obeyed by screaming "YAHHHHHH!" at the top of his little lungs.

Well, that worked, Hanazuki thought, climbing

out from beneath most of the fruit so she could cover her ears, if nothing else.

In a flash, Dazzlessence Jones was racing toward them. He was so shiny, it was blinding. Like a diamond skier, he dug the edges of his cowboy boots into the moon's surface to skid to a stop, clouding Hanazuki and Lime Green in moon soot. When the air cleared, he had his badge out. It read: MOON SHERIFF, CRIME HATER AKA CRATER, AND THE MOON'S MOST SHINY. "Hey *yo*! Did someone say, 'YAHHHHHH?'"

Hanazuki, in no mood for small talk, just pointed up.

Dazzlessence glanced at the sky and gasped. "*Goodness gracious, great balls of fire!* What're you doing comet-gazing, Hanazuki? There's no time for that! This is a disaster waiting to happen."

"I don't think the disaster's waiting," she said flatly.

"You're right. Let's stop those *great balls of fire* before they make *one great ball of fire* that destroys us all. You *in*?"

"Inner than in!" Hanazuki stood up with so much oomph that the rest of the fruit flew from her body. "What's the plan, Sheriff?"

"To the Safety Cave! *Woooo-eeeee!* This is *NOT A DRILL*!"

About the Author

Stacy Davidowitz is an author, playwright, and screenwriter based in Manhattan. Her book babies include *Camp Rolling Hills, Crossing Over, Breakout!* and *Freefall.* When she's not writing, you can find her teaching creative writing and theater, running long distances, and singing show tunes. Visit her at stacydavidowitz.com.

About the Illustrator

Victoria Ying is a rare native Angeleno. She started her career in the arts by falling in love with comic books. This eventually turned into a career working in animation. She loves Japanese curry, putting things in her online shopping cart and taking them out again, and hanging out with her dopey dog. Her book credits include *Meow!*; *Not Quite Black and White*; *Lost and Found, What's That Sound?*; and *Unicorn Magic.*